Anonymous

Rachel

Or, the city without walls

Anonymous

Rachel
Or, the city without walls

ISBN/EAN: 9783337042257

Printed in Europe, USA, Canada, Australia, Japan

Cover: Foto ©Andreas Hilbeck / pixelio.de

More available books at **www.hansebooks.com**

RACHEL;

OR,

THE CITY WITHOUT W

PORTER,

CONTENTS.

Illustrations.

THE CITY WITHOUT WALLS.

CHAPTER I.

HOW RACHEL LEARNS TO PRAY.

RACHEL stood at the window and watched Ernest on the morning when he left the Asylum with his new father, until he could no longer be seen. Then she stole away into the darkest, stillest corner of the school-room, and hid her face. She did not shed a tear; she only put her hands closely together and shut her eyes very tight. For some reason the sun-light was not pleasant, and the happy

voices of the children sounded noisily.
No one noticed her. She heard Miss
Camp calling the classes to order, and
the tramp of little feet crossing the
uncarpeted floor. Ernest's class in
spelling was the first to recite. Rachel waited, almost hoping to hear
the quick response of his voice; but
no, it was only Teddy Scott; and he
missed, which Ernest never did.

"I hope," said Miss Camp, "my
little scholars will take a great deal
of pains to get their lessons well, that
I may not wish Ernest back for his
good example. Which of you boys
is going to take his place as leader of
the class?"

"I am going to try," said Christie.

Rachel shook her head very impatiently, and felt as if she wanted to
shake Christie too.

"I hope you will. If you try Christie, you can do almost anything; but you must remember how faithfully Ernest studied. He did not look on his book one moment, and all around the school-room the next."

"No, but he drawed ships. I saw him lots of times," said Christie, archly. ·

"He never did!" said Rachel sharply.

"Rachel," said Miss Camp, "that is not a polite or pleasant way of speaking. I am sorry you should do so."

Now Rachel was not in a mood to bear reproof. She was feeling very unhappy without quite knowing the reason why, and so she said more rudely still,

"I don't care; I hate him. He

always thinks he can do everything, and he aint half so good as Ernest."

" Go to your room, and stay there until you feel willing to behave like a good girl," said Miss Camp.

Rachel put her head down on the desk again and did not move. Miss Camp waited a few minutes. She knew Rachel's bad temper so well that she almost dreaded to come into contact with it, and she knew too that this freak of ill-humor had come only from grief at parting with Ernest; still, the outbreak had been so rude and uncalled-for that it would not do to pass it over un-noticed. The eyes of all the other children were upon her, and among such an assembly it was very neces-sary to preserve discipline. She knew too that Rachel's temper though hasty, was not lasting. A few minutes of quiet would often entirely subdue her. So she waited patiently, but did not go on with her class. The school-room was very still; you could have heard a pin drop. They did hear Rachel breathing heavily, as if she were all ready to burst into a loud fit of weeping.

Miss Camp hoped for that result. Rachel would then be tender and more easily reached. But no, the very hush in the room only goaded her on, made her more angry and more uncomfortable.

"Rachel!" There was something in Miss Camp's voice which made the other children start, but Rachel did not move; so the teacher walked across the room and laid her hand very gently on the dark curls.

"Poor little Rachel," she said, and the authority in her voice had changed to great tenderness, " I am very sorry you feel so badly. We shall all of us miss Ernest, but it wont bring him back to be naughty, and say unkind things. You would not like to have him know you were disobeying and grieving me, would you ?"

The teacher's hand soothed the throbbing nerves of the child even more than the kind words. " Now I will let you sit here a few minutes longer, if you think you can come like a good child, and tell Christie you are sorry for what you have said; then you would like to go to your room and ask God to forgive you, and give you better control over your quick temper, wouldn't you ?"

There was no answer, but the

quick breathing grew calmer. Miss Camp hoped she had gained an easy victory this time, but she did not like to leave Rachel, and she was wondering what she could do when she saw Faith making her way quietly toward her seat. How pale she was! any little excitement told so quickly on the delicate child. She came noiselessly in to the desk, and sat down by Rachel's side. Then she put up her little hand, so little and wan, beside Miss Camp's. Rachel started; she knew the touch at once, but she had not heard Faith come. Pretty soon Faith put her cheek down, and Miss Camp drew her hand away and went back to her class. There was something in Faith's earnest face which told her that she could be spared. The chil

dren all seemed to understand that
the matter was settled, and that it
was only now a question of time; it
would be right in the end. The spelling was resumed, and by the time the
lesson was finished, Rachel had put
her arm around Faith, and the part
of the desk upon which she laid her
head was wet with tears.

"Now, Rachel," whispered Faith
softly as the children were going to
their seats, "there is Christie coming
right by. He is such a darling, you
wouldn't make him feel bad for the
world. Tell him so when he comes.
That is what Christie May would call
being generous."

Rachel sat up very straight and
looked Christie steadily in the face
as he came toward her. Such a
happy, hearty face, no one could look

long into it without catching some of
the sunny temper that made it so
pleasant. "A merry heart doeth
good like a medicine." If Faith's
loving ways had helped Rachel to
try to do right at first, Christie's
smile finished the work; and when
he was near enough to speak to him,
she said,

"I am sorry, Christie, I spoke so
cross to you."

"O I don't mind, Rachie, I am
cross as two sticks myself sometimes,
and then I would bite a board nail
in two, I dare say, if I had one between my teeth;" and Christie snap-
ped two rows of very white little
teeth, as if he were anxious to make
the experiment, though he was laughing all the time.

Rachel laughed too, so did Faith,

and Miss Camp saw that the troubled
waters were once more at rest.

Now would Rachel go to her room
and ask God to forgive her? Faith
was anxious that she should, and so
she whispered, with that peculiarly
beautiful expression in her large eyes
which God had given to her, to com-
pensate in part for the many things
of which he had deprived her, "Now
Jesus is just as ready as Christie was.
Come, Rachel, then you can be all
happy," and she slid off from her
seat and held out her hand. Rachel
almost mechanically put hers in it,
and suffered herself to be led away.
Miss Camp smiled as they passed
her, and said, "For thou, Lord, art
good and ready to forgive, and plen-
teous in mercy unto all them that
call upon thee."

Now when Rachel had reached her room and Faith had shut the door and left her alone, my young readers must not suppose that she knelt down and repeated a little prayer. Rachel was not a praying child. She had been taught to say the Lord's prayer before she came to the Asylum, and since then she had learned several other appropriate child's prayers; but Rachel never thought much about God or Jesus, never felt that she was at times a sinful little child, and needed forgiveness and a blessing. She was so strong and well and full of life that she only minded what was passing before her; what she could see and hear and feel. Her conscience was not tender. She never thought whether a thing was right or wrong, only whether she wished or did not wish to do it, and she indulged her high temper at all times with *as little attempt at self-control as if she were not capable of it.

It was in vain that good Aunty May time after time pointed out to her how wrong this was. Not a day passed but in some way it was roused and made trouble for herself and all around her. After trying various modes of punishment, the matron had decided that there was none so effectual as to leave her alone. She also faithfully tried to impress upon her the need of asking the forgiveness of that Friend, so much greater than any earthly friend, whom she had grieved. But if Rachel had wished to pray, she would not have known how, and this was a point

which had never occurred to the matron.   If she could have looked at
Rachel now, as she stood in the middle of the room, with her eyes fixed
upon the floor and a sad expression
on her face, she would, notwithstanding all her experience with children,
have learned a new lesson.   Rachel
did not know, if she knelt down and
only said, "Now I lay me," or "Jesus,
gentle shepherd, hear me," that it
would be asking the great God to
forgive her for being cross and quick
tempered, just as much as if she had
said, "O, God, please to forgive me
for being angry and having spoken
cross to Christie, for Christ's sake."
God could look right into her heart
and would know just what she
meant even better than she knew
herself, and he would see that she

was sorry and wanted to be forgiven
No one had ever explained to her
the nature of prayer, and that God
had made her mind for it as much as
he had made her eyes to see the light,
and her ears to hear the birds sing,
and her mouth to taste nice fruit.
So here she stood to-day looking
down on the floor in a very troubled,
bewildered kind of a way. Perhaps
there were some thoughts down at
the bottom of her heart which God
could read, and which he accepted
for a prayer. No one can tell. Certain it is that Rachel wished to be
good, and hoped never, never to be
angry again so long as she lived. If
she had been older she could have
reasoned more; but we must not forget how young she was, and then we
do not know that she had religious

parents. It does not seem that she had ever heard her mother pray. I am sure that every one of my little readers who has a praying mother will know how to pray better than Rachel did; for you will remember what words she used when she brought you to the throne of grace and pleaded for you, that some sin might be blotted out from the great book forever. Let me say to those children who have not been so blessed, When you want to pray, do not think of God, with his angels around him, as a being a long way off in heaven, and too busy and too great to mind what a little child says. To-day he is in the room with Rachel. He is listening to hear the least word she shall utter. He cares as much for her, poor orphan and pauper child as she is, as he would if she were the single one in all his wide world, and he had nothing else to do but save and bless her. So you must remember, when you wish to pray, that God is there with you, not away off in some dim, distant place that you cannot. even imagine. And then there is one other thing; when you pray tell him the truth. Do not think that you can deceive him. It is not prayer if your lips use words which your heart does not feel. It is not important that you should have a set form of speech, it is only needful that you should be in earnest to have God to love you, and Jesus take you in his arms and bless you.

There was once a little boy who had done wrong. He was a gentle, loving child, and he was grieved over his sin, so at night, just before he went to bed, he knelt down by his crib, and folding his hands, he said,

"O, Jesus, please lub me, and I will try to be dood morrow-day." Then feeling that that was not quite enough, he knelt again, and said, "And please lub my little gray kitty, the one with white ears, for Christ's sake. Amen."

Those were true prayers, for the boy's heart was in them. He loved his kitten best of anything in the world, and he felt that in some way he gave it to Jesus, and that to give it was to show him how much he wished to love him, and to be good.

Now the point of this first chapter is this, I want you to notice it par-ticularly, for a great deal of the in-

terest and value of this book will
depend upon it : Rachel's chief fault
was an ungoverned, high temper.
She was handsome, as you will remember, with very large dark eyes,
and long, glossy black curls. She
was bright and quick at her lessons,
and had many smart and pleasant
ways about her, so that no one could
be long with her without loving her.
Her manners, too, were generally
winning. She was thoughtful for
others, and thoughtless about herself; that is, she was not strongly
selfish, never wanted the best, and
she was as contented in seeing others
happy as in being happy herself.
But with all these charming things
everybody had some fear of her.
No one in the Asylum was long with
her without watching her moods,

and being very careful not to do anything to offend her. This was because she became so quickly and so fearfully angry. Sometimes it was one thing which annoyed her, sometimes it was another, but scarcely a day passed during which she did not give way to her temper. This was a very bad and troublesome trait, one which caused Aunty May much annoyance, and over which, so far, she had been able to exercise very little control. The only one in the Asylum, now that Ernest was gone, who would be likely to help her was Faith, and she was never present at one of Rachel's outbreaks without suffering from it afterward in nervous debility or renewed attacks of pain.

When Aunty May found that weeks

and months passed on without any obvious change for the better in Rachel in this respect, she began to fall back upon what was always her last as well as her first resort: prayer. She prayed, and used every means her experience and observation could suggest; and when she found the means only seemed to make matters worse, she trusted only to prayer. How great and sufficient an aid it is even in our direst needs. The struggle which Rachel had, both before and after she learned how to pray, will be shown in a few words in the following pages. God will help those who ask him in a simple, childlike, earnest, truthful way. Every one of these words are important in their meaning. Ponder them well, young reader, and at the same time ask God to explain and impress them upon your hearts.

Rachel remained where she was until she had prayed and had been heard, as we will hope. When Aunty May came to bring her down to the school-room, she found there a gentle child, with a softened look in her eyes, and she felt sorry for her as she saw the almost discouraged expression with which she received the few words of tender reproof that she felt it her duty to give.

"Dear Rachel," she said, "it is very hard, I know it is, but God will help you."

Faith was waiting for her near the door. Miss Camp had just called out the geography class, a study of which Rachel was very fond, and in studying which she often helped both

Faith and Christie. This lesson had
been very interesting; so many odd
places to find, and all on the bright-
colored maps. These three children
learned it well, and Miss Camp
praised them warmly, so warmly,
that Rachel's heart, which had felt
so heavy and sad, began to be lighter
and happier; and when she went
back to her seat, no one would have
recognized her as the same child who
had so recently wet the lid of the
desk with her angry tears. Christie
had unconsciously taken Ernest's va-
cant seat; he even had his slate and
pencil in his hand, and now he was
marking over a half-rubbed-out ship
which Ernest had drawn the day
before. Rachel watched him eagerly. How many ships Ernest had
drawn for her, how many times he

had given her his slate and pencil,
and laughed at her awkward attempts to imitate him. Where was
he now? Would he never come
back again? Would that great man
with the black hat be kind to him?
Would he miss her, and want to see
her as much as she did him? Who
was Ally? A little new sister? Rachel sat and silently thought over
these things, while Christie drew his
ship. Faith played with her great rag
doll, and the other children, freed
from the restraints of school, frolick-
ed around the room, as happy and
full of life and joy, as if they were in
their own homes, and not members
of only a charity Orphan Asylum; but
they were Christ's dear lambs even
here.

CHAPTER II.

RACHEL GOES HOME.

Mrs. Tilton's interest in the Orphan Asylum had been very much freshened since she had placed Rachel there. She now went to visit it every week, and the child became constantly nearer and dearer to her. She was pleased with her progress in almost every particular. Her lessons were always well reported, she had learned to sew neatly, and her little habits, many of which had become careless from neglect, were fast becoming ladylike. The matron made no secret to Mrs. Tilton of the temper which gave her so much trouble. She frequently went to her for ad-

and Mrs. Tilton was both surprised and grieved at the frequency
and violence of its appearance. So
far, however, in her intercourse with
Rachel she had not attempted to use
any direct influence over her for the
purpose of preventing it. She knew
that with so young a child it would
do very little good to reason or to
exact from her a promise of care-
fulness for the future. Rachel's temper was born in her. It was as natural as her propensity to eat or
drink, to laugh or cry, to be pleased
or sorry, and she was scarcely able
to check it; but it was necessary
that she should be taught to over-
come it. She must learn the way to
ask help from God, as well as to read,
to sew, to study, or any other of the
many things children have to learn.

Mrs. Tilton thought it would be less to rebuke Rachel in her happy moments for a fault committed in the past, and it strangely happened that often as she saw Rachel, and frequent as the bursts of childish temper were, she had never witnessed one of them.

It was singular how, from the very first moment of her being released from the police officer, Rachel had clung to Mrs. Tilton. She always came down into the parlor (no longer, thanks to her benefactress, so desolate as it was on the morning when she was first brought there,) with such a happy face, that its memory staid with the kind lady long afterward. To sit close by her side, with both of her little hands clasping tight the gloved one that

was always ready for her; to fix her
eyes on Mrs. Tilton's face with such
longing, loving look; seemed to
make her perfectly happy. Mrs.
Tilton almost always brought her a
little present, but while she remained
that was of small value to Rachel.
It would drop upon the floor, be
thrown carelessly upon a chair, indeed, be quite forgotten until the
giver was gone. Then she rarely
parted with it for a moment, until at
night sleep had made both the gift
and the visit seem like things of the
past.

This was unusual in such a child.
Aunty May wondered over it, and
Mrs. Tilton could not forget it, even
after leaving the asylum. It did not
occur to any of them then that this
was one way in which God was keep-

ing his promise of remembering the fatherless; but it certainly was.

Soon after Ernest left for his home on Nelson's Island, Aunty May began to find the care of Rachel, without his controlling influence, too much for her, and she felt that it would be necessary to find a home for her also as soon as possible. Not a day passed now but there was trouble somewhere. One day Rachel pushed a boy down stairs, hurting him quite severely, because he had knocked carelessly against Faith as she was coming slowly and painfully up. At another time she struck Janet Dodge in her mouth, causing swollen lips and bleeding teeth. Teddy Jones was hurled against the hot stove for taking Ernest's slate away from Christie. In short, if either Miss

Camp or Aunty May heard a sudden cry of pain or fear, they never doubted that it was caused by Rachel. One of the most trying things of all was, that Rachel was seldom made angry by any indignity or injury offered to herself; it was always for something done to some one she loved, so it was very difficult to know just how to blame her. But the constant care and anxiety which she occasioned were very severe upon those who had the charge of her; besides, the discipline of the whole Asylum was injured. Children who were hasty, but much better able to control themselves than poor Rachel, made less attempt to do so. They took advantage of the leniency which Aunty May was in a measure obliged to show to her; and so, before Rachel had been in the Asylum three months, it became a different place from what it was when she entered. Lest my readers may not observe the truth which this fact so clearly shows I will stop here and point it out. Don't you see how that fault of yours, for which your parents have reproved you so often, does not affect you alone? Every one of your family suffers with you, and not only your own family, but the school of which you are a member, and through the school, the whole neighborhood in which you live. O, child, you are small and young, but you are of great importance, and can do for good or for ill as much as many a grown person. Remember this when you carelessly do not take any pains to correct a fault. You must not

only suffer and be punished for it
yourself, but you make others suffer
too. Does that seem generous or
kind-hearted in you?

During one of Mrs. Tilton's visits,
before Rachel was called in, Aunty
May discussed the subject of a new
home with her. She felt that in a
very eminent degree the influence
under which Rachel might fall would
form her character, and that therefore it would be necessary to exercise
extreme caution in its selection. The
uncommon beauty of the child had
already attracted much attention
from the visitors of the Asylum, and
several had wished to adopt her; but
Aunty May had always answered,
"that she was not ready to part with
the child." Indeed, while she felt
that the good of all required that

she should leave, her future seemed
very hopeless; so she could only
commend her to her kind Father in
heaven, and trust her to him. Aunty
May often said that she never prayed
so much for any other of the hund-
reds of children who had been under
her care as she did for Rachel, and
she never felt more sure that God
had heard and answered.

Mrs. Tilton also had been feeling
for some time that the Asylum was
no place for such a child as Rachel.
She needed more care, a stronger and
more immediate personal discipline
than she could find as one among so
many; but what could be done with
her? Mrs. Tilton had numerous
persons dependent upon her charity,
but there was not one among them
all who seemed so peculiarly her

charge as Rachel had from the moment she stopped her carriage opposite the frightened, screaming child
on the sidewalk until the present;
and this new home, therefore, she
determined to find; but where?
There was no one among the circle
of her friends who would be likely
to adopt the child of unknown parents, picked up in the street, and
carried to an Orphan Asylum, and it
would be equally difficult to find any
one fitted for the trust. It was
weeks before it ever occurred to her
that perhaps God was calling her to
that task, and even then it did not
immediately assume the form of im-
perative duty.

It need hardly now be told the
reader that Mrs. Tilton belonged to
that large class of wealthy people to

whom God has not only given the means, but also the will and the power to do a great deal of good. She had generally found enough to occupy her outside of her own home; this she had held sacred to its own enjoyments and memories. She was a lady of much cultivation, moving in the midst of a large and influential literary circle, with her time and thoughts so fully occupied that it seemed to those looking on impossible to find room for anything more. But Mrs. Tilton was more than wealthy and benevolent. She was a warm-hearted, sincere, active Christian, feeling that her time, her money, and her health were given to her to use, first of all, in her Master's service. The world knew her for a large-hearted, benevolent lady; God knew her for an humble, faithful worker in his vineyard.

Some years previous to the period of which we are speaking she had lost, within a few months of each other, her two children; but she had not for this reason allowed herself to feel that the only duty which remained to her in life was to suffer passively. She knew they were safe "in the garden of her Lord," and if she meekly bore her cross, she should one day find them waiting for her there. But their memories were very precious to her, and she had never felt inclined to take others in their stead. The first thought of adopting Rachel was, therefore, one of great pain. She could not hear the dear word "mother" spoken by other

lips than those now so still and cold,
and yet she would not wrong one of
Jesus's little ones by taking it to a
home from which she withheld the
heart. But with every sight of Rachel, since it was determined that
she must leave the Asylum, came the
thought, pressing closer and closer
upon her conscience, of her own
ability and duty to do what there
seemed no one else so well qualified
to attempt.

Her husband at first met the proposition with a decided refusal. She
had already as much care as her
health would allow; the child could
be sent to some pleasant country
home, and, if necessary, he would
put aside every year a certain sum
for her support; but he had no fancy
for such a new element in his family;

indeed, it was not to be thought of
for a moment.

But Mrs. Tilton knew that this was
out of consideration for herself more
than from any other motive, as he was
very fond of children, and had not
struggled back into life from the
graves of his own lost ones with half
her quiet resignation. And as she
every day became more and more
convinced that she ought to take
Rachel, she at last won from him a
reluctant consent to make the trial.
He had never seen her, but had always been interested in what Mrs.
Tilton had told him of her. It must
be acknowledged now, however, that
he shrank very much from the under-
taking, and would gladly have paid
a large sum to any one to relieve
them from the seeming duty.

The struggle through which Mrs. Tilton had passed had not been made known to any one but her husband. It was, therefore, no wonder that Aunty May thought God had directly answered her prayer when she said to her that she, herself, had resolved to adopt Rachel.

No one could see the tears that would rush into Aunty May's eyes and roll down her cheeks, and hear how fervently she said, "May the orphan's God bless you, dear lady," without being convinced that this good matron was well adapted to her place, and that she truly loved those who were intrusted to her care.

There was not a day to be lost. If Rachel was to come, the sooner the better; so that very morning she

bade good-by to the children and to
the matron, and with great, wondering eyes took her seat as the rich lady's child in her elegant carriage.

Faith threw both her puny arms
around her neck, and sobbed aloud.
How could she part with her! She
had always been good and kind to her;
never angry with her, never forgetful
of her. Must everybody whom she
loved go away? Had God no little
sick Faith in his world; only the well,
handsome children that he could care
for? Was she always, always to be
left, and always to have such a dull,
aching heart and body? Faith did
not ask herself all these questions as
she hung around Rachel's neck; but
she sobbed, and wished it was night
and dark, so that she could be alone
and still, and then somehow go away

out of life, and not be here any more.
But that night, when it grew dark
and cold, and there was no Rachel to
pull the small wadded sack up over
her aching shoulders, or make Janet
give up the easy chair, which Mrs.
Tilton had bought to rest her spine,
then she thought all these other
things; and she could not answer
them, neither could she tell them to
Aunty May. She could have told
them to her mother, but, alas! to no
one else.

Christie was half glad and half
sorry to have Rachel go. He loved
her when she was quiet and pleasant,
but he had too many memories of
knocks and pinches from her when
he was angry to really care for her.
thought several of the other girls
much better, and they made him

happier; so he said good-by quite in-
differently, and climbed up on the
window-sill to watch the handsome
horses, as he always did when he
knew Mrs. Tilton's carriage was at the
door. John, the coachman, had learned to know his chubby, pleasant face,
and always looked for it; indeed, here
began an acquaintance which ripened
into a warm affection in after life.

Rachel was silent as they drove
through the noisy streets; perhaps
she remembered her other ride there,
and was thinking of the life from
which she had then been rescued; perhaps she was wondering about the
new home to which she was going.
Mrs. Tilton thought, as she watched
her, that she would like to know of
what she was thinking, but she did
not speak to her until the carriage

stopped before her own door. So
far she had not said to Rachel that
she intended to take her for her own.
She felt that her husband must be
the one, in the end, to decide the
question, and if he should dislike the
child, it would be wrong for her to
insist on her remaining, so she had
told her she was to go home with
her, without entering into particulars,
nor is it to be supposed that Rachel
attached any special meaning to the
plan.

There was still another important
member of Mrs. Tilton's family whom,
for many reasons, it was very desirable to please in the matter of adopting Rachel. This was an old serv-
ant, Nancy Pratt. Nancy had been
in the family of Mrs. Tilton's mother
for many years before coming into

hers, and had been a kind of mother to her all her life. She was a woman of very decided character, and not always easy to please. She was neat to a fault, careful and painstaking, and very easily put out of humor by anything which interfered with order and propriety. She had a cross way of speaking, too, which irritated those who did not know her; in short, with a great many good and noble traits, Nancy was not one of those persons who would be chosen to live with if it could be helped. She was fond of children and, in her way, indulgent to them; but it was only when they did not by deed or look cross or annoy her. If they succeeded in getting on her right side—and very distinct the sides were—they might be comfortable and happy, but if they were on the wrong side, there would be no rest for them in her presence.

Mrs. Tilton had no trouble with her, and she found her extremely useful. She had so much good sense and shrewdness, that she could be trusted almost anywhere to do what was to be done, though it was not always accomplished to the satisfaction or happiness of all concerned.

She had always been interested in Rachel; she had made many of the clothes which Mrs. Tilton had prepared for her, and had, perhaps, been consulted more than any one else, besides Mr. Tilton, as to receiving her into the family. Much to Mrs. Tilton's surprise she said that she considered it her "bounden duty;" and when a thing was a bounden duty, why, the Lord meant that it should take place, and that was just the reason why he had laid it on her. If he saw fit to take their own precious lambs from them, that was not any reason why the good fold should be desolate. For her part, she would rather hear a child's voice around the house and little pattering feet going up and down, than any of your grand piannies, she did not care who played them. And this was the way Nancy Pratt felt in the morning when Rachel was brought home.

She was peeping through the window-blind of the room which used to be the nursery when the carriage stopped. Many tears and heart-aches it cost both Mrs. Tilton and Nancy to open this desolated room again, but, firm in her resolve not to shrink

4

from anything which promised the good of the child, Mrs. Tilton had not hesitated. She knew that one of the first things requisite for the happiness of children, is a place peculiarly their own, where they can be free to move and act as they please, and in a house as handsomely furnished and nicely kept as her own this was specially desirable. Nancy had taken out some of May's toys; they had been put away so sacredly since the dear child last played with them, that they looked almost new to her now. New, and yet how many old, old thoughts clustered around them. May had been an angel five long years, it almost seemed to Nancy as if she had gone when she, too, was a child, and that somehow when she saw her once more she should be a

child again, and they should play together. John lifted Rachel out in
his arms, and put her tenderly down
upon the steps. Rachel raised her
eyes to look at the house and met
those of Nancy looking down upon
her.

" Brown as a chestnut," said Nancy aloud to herself; " no more like
our May than nothing, but it's all
the better for that. The poor, dear,
motherless little thing that she is, and
such a beauty too !"

Rachel had never been within such
a house before, but her hand was now
in Mrs. Tilton's, and she would have
followed her anywhere. Now she
goes through the long entry, up, up,
the soft, flower-carpeted stairs, seeing everything and trembling a little,
just a little, at so much new beauty ;

and then Mrs. Tilton opens the door, and says to Nancy, who had been listening as they came, "Nancy, this is our little Rachel."

CHAPTER III.

RACHEL'S CANARIES, AND WHAT THEY BRING.

RACHEL had never heard of fairy palaces, as I presume most of my readers have; but if she had, she would certainly have thought she was dropped down into one now. Such a contrast as this nursery was to the bare, though cheerful school-room at the Asylum! Mrs. Tilton had taken a great deal of pains to make it tasteful and cheerful for her own children, and it was none the less so for the new-found child of to-day. A pretty paper, gay with bright flowers, covered the walls, and other flowers smiled up to her from the carpet under her feet. It seemed

to the dazzled and bewildered child
that it was flowers everywhere, for on
the mantle-piece Nancy had arranged
pretty vases filled from the conserva-
tory, and in the window two pots held
large blossoming shrubs.   Nancy herself, so neat and prim, so homely, and
yet looking so kindly, came to meet
her with outstretched arms, and the
first thing Rachel heard her say was:

"God be thanked for giving this
lonely old heart a young child to
love again!"

Rachel did not understand her;
she only knew that she kissed her several times, and that for some reason
she put her own arms round Nancy's
neck as she never had dared to do
around Mrs. Tilton's, and laid her little round cheek down on the withered,
tear-stained one of the old woman,

and could not look away from the love that shone out of her eyes, even to the beautiful flowers which were all around her.

Mrs. Tilton drew a long breath of relief. So far all was well: Nancy had certainly taken a fancy to the child. Now if Rachel, like May, was only one of the gentle ones: but she was not, and Nancy's own temper had not improved from age. Still, as it would do no good to borrow trouble, Mrs. Tilton determined to be satisfied with what was hopeful in to-day, and to leave to-morrow in the hands of Him who careth for us. One would have thought, to see Rachel and Nancy together now, that Rachel was a long absent one returned, rather than an orphan child brought to a new home.

Clothes which were suitable for the change in the circumstances of her life had been prepared for Rachel, and Nancy's first act of care was to dress her neatly in them. If she had thought her pretty before, her admiration now was but ill disguised, and it was difficult for even Mrs. Tilton to restrain showing how pleased and surprised she was at the change which the dress wrought. If Mr. Tilton also would be pleased with the appearance and manners of the child, she felt as if the most difficult part of the adoption was passed.

Rachel was to dine to-day in the nursery with Nancy. Mrs. Tilton was very particular about the table manners of a child, and she very well knew Rachel would need much instruction.

Mr. Tilton's first inquiry on his return was if Rachel had been brought, and when he was told that she was in the nursery, he went directly there to see her.

Mrs. Tilton heard him ascending the stairs, and knew the anxiety which prompted him. Nancy, too, heard him coming, and all the nice lesson which she had intended to give Rachel in order to prepare her for the meeting were lost; but she said, " There is Mr. Tilton; now, Rachel, you must behave like a little lady;" and like a little lady surely Rachel did behave. She went to him the moment he called her, and though she looked very searchingly in his face, as she had in that of the others, still she answered his questions promptly and so modestly that Mr.

Tilton was well pleased. He talked with her a few minutes, then stopped at his wife's door as he went down.

"Well?" she said, looking up anxiously.

"I like the child; she has mind and beauty. The latter is of no value without the other, but both together are rare."

"I am very glad that she pleases you."

"So am I. We will do our best to give the orphan a good home."

And so Rachel was adopted.

The change in the child's life for a time acted very favorably, so far as any exhibition of her temper was concerned. Away from all other children, she had now no occasion for being angry; there was nothing to try or annoy her. Mrs. Tilton was decided, but so gentle in what she required that it was pleasant to obey her, and as for Nancy, the only danger so far was from her unlimited indulgence of all the child's wishes.

Feeling desirous that Rachel should be well grounded in all the rudiments of learning, Mrs. Tilton spent an hour every morning in her instruction, and Nancy taught her the use of her needle in the very nice, old-time way of sewing. Rachel was quick, and willing to learn, and by the time she had been a month in the house Mrs. Tilton wondered she ever could have hesitated to adopt so good and so uncommon a child.

Mrs. Tilton brought her home a great many presents, and among them were two canaries. One of them was called Dick. He had golden wings, with just a tiny white spot on his breast. The other was Nellie. She had some pretty brown feathers on the tips of her wings, and a brown tail. They were in a white and blue cage, and when Nancy hung it in the window, and Dick began to sing, Rachel was a very happy child. She could not learn her spelling, she could not even sew, though Nancy, seeing how full she was of her treasures, thoughtfully changed the hour's occupation. Rachel could do nothing but stand up in a chair, close to the cage, and watch the little things while they jumped from their perch to the floor of the cage, picking a seed out from the well-filled glass, eating it so daintily, and then dipping their round heads into the clear water and lifting them up again with such a happy, satisfied look in their brown eyes.

If Nancy had realized that Rachel had never before seen a canary or any other kind of a bird nearer than upon the limbs of the trees on the common, she would have been even more considerate than she was, and would have taken away all tasks for this morning; but this never occurred to her. May had owned birds; they had swung from that very nail in the window all her short life, and Nancy thought they were as much a part of a little girl's happiness as her doll. So now, after having spoken kindly several times to Rachel to induce her to go back to her sewing, she said at last sharply,

"Let them birds alone, Rachel

Tilton, and go back to your patchwork."

Not an inch did Rachel move
She never even took her eyes from
the cage ; and Nancy, after watching
her for a moment, with an ominous
frown gathering between her eye-
brows, said again,

" Don't you hear me ? Let them
alone ; you wont have a walk with
me on the common one step till that
whole square is done."

If Rachel had been stone deaf she
could not have shown less attention.
Nancy caught her arm quickly,
and, without thinking much of dislo-
cated shoulders, landed her on the
floor. Rachel flew at her, struck,
scratched, pinched, and bit her, much
more like an enraged animal than
like a child. At first Nancy was too

much surprised to make any resistance, and it was not until she felt
Rachel's teeth in the fleshy part of
her thumb that she tried to defend
herself, and even then it required all
the exercise of her strength to hold
and control her.

Mrs. Tilton heard from her room
the screams with which Rachel vent-
ed her fury, and Nancy's loud and
angry rebukes, and, hastening in,
found Rachel struggling in Nancy's
firm grasp, with her face purple with
anger, and Nancy with an expression
of mingled terror and vexation.

To separate the two was no easy
task. Words of command and en-
treaty proved at first in vain; and it
was not until Mrs. Tilton had her
hand fairly over Rachel's mouth that
she could stop either her screams or

her attempts to bite. But at last Rachel's eyes, so wild and unnatural in their staring expression, began to droop a little, and the rigid muscles to yield. Mrs. Tilton took the tight-clenched hands in hers, and held them gently; and Nancy, with a great effort, yielded the child to her mistress.

" O, ma'am," she said, catching her breath as she spoke, "if she be'ent a tiger, a real lion, then I never saw nor heard any one who was; why she is a wild-cat. See here how she clawed me;" and Nancy held out her scratched and bleeding hands.

" What does this all mean, Nancy ?"

" Just nothing at all, ma'am. She wanted to look at them birds long past her lesson time, and I thought as they were new it was natural like, and so I told her to take her sewing instead — you know she could hear them sing and sew too; but when I spoke to her she didn't take no more notice of me than just nothing at all, and I spoke again, and she was as deaf as a post; so I took hold of her and put her down here, and she flew at me."

Nancy, as she told the story, cast many angry and revengeful looks at Rachel, who stood close by Mrs. Tilton's side, looking from one to the other, as if she had just waked from a dream, a bad, ugly dream.

Mrs. Tilton saw the expression, the same that she had seen on the day of the street affray. She remembered then that she had been able to soothe her only by the most tender treatment,

and that, of course, was the best way
now; so she said to Nancy, " You
may go, Nancy, I will talk with you
more by and by when she is quieter."

Nancy looked as if she wanted to
question the order, and have the
trouble settled then and there; but a
look from Mrs. Tilton told her that
there was no use in disputing it, and
she very reluctantly moved away.

Mrs. Tilton sat down in the rocking chair, the very one in which she
had so often rocked her own children
to sleep, and laying Rachel's head
upon her breast, without saying one
word, she began to rock her. As
she did so, God sent into her heart
so many sweet, motherly thoughts,
so many memories, gentle and tender, that the wild throbbing pulses
that were beating against hers could

not but be stilled. After a few minutes' silence, she began to sing a soft, low lullaby, one which she had sung so many, many times before; and as she sung, Rachel's quick breathing became more quiet, her mouth partly opened, and soon her head, which had only staid where Mrs. Tilton had placed it, because she felt that it must, drooped heavily. The storm was past. The child remained quiet so long that Mrs. Tilton thought she must have fallen asleep; and when she looked down into her face, she was surprised to see her wide awake, and with a loving look in her eyes.

"Dear little Rachel," she said; "you are very sorry that you have done so wrong."

Rachel nestled closer to her, but did not speak.

"Do you know whom you have made sorry besides mamma," (Rachel called Mrs. Tilton mamma now,) "and papa, and good, kind Nancy, and little Rachel?"

"No, mamma," said Rachel in a whisper.

"You have grieved your dear Saviour."

Rachel looked up wonderingly.

"Listen to me, Rachel. You remember last night I told you about Jesus taking the little children in his arms and blessing them, and how he was waiting to love and bless you?"

"And did he come and stay in my room all night after you went away?" asked Rachel quickly.

"Yes, when papa and mamma and Nancy were asleep too, and there was no one to take care of you,

Jesus was there, and he kept all harm away, and when you were rested he sent the morning light and the bright sun to wake you and make you happy and good all day."

"When did he go away?"

"He has never gone away; he was here when papa brought home the pretty birds, and he loved to see them and to have you happy with them."

"Where is he now?"

"He is here, and he was here when you were so very wicked. He saw it all; he saw how you struck and pinched and bit; he saw every print which your teeth made in Nancy's hands, and every drop of blood which your nails drew. How do you think he felt?"

Rachel sat up and looked searchingly round in the room, then turned her eyes with a doubting expression toward her new mother.

Mrs. Tilton understood it, and said, "You think, perhaps, because you cannot see him that he is not here. You know I have always told you no one could see God, or Christ, until they die and go to heaven. When I came into your room last night after dark and spoke to you behind the curtains of your bed, and you answered me, could you see me?"

"No, mamma."

"And yet you knew I was there and was speaking to you?"

"Yes, mamma."

"It is just so with Jesus. He is here, but you cannot see him any more than you could see me, because he is a spirit, and that shuts him out from your sight just as much as the dark shuts me out. Now, as he loves you better than any one else can, so he feels more grieved and sorry when you do wrong than even I do."

"I don't believe it," said Rachel.

"Rachel, that is a very improper way of speaking."

"But I don't want him to be sorry, and to love me better than you do. I love you best."

Mrs. Tilton saw this was a point it would be in vain to argue with her now, so she said, "I hope I love Jesus a great deal better than I do any one else, and there is no one I am so sorry to grieve. When I have done wrong the first thing I do is to kneel down and ask him to forgive me; so now we will kneel down and I will ask him to forgive my child and

make her better. I am going to tell
him just what a naughty, wicked
temper she has, and ask him to help
her to govern it."

Without saying any more Mrs.
Tilton knelt by the rocking chair,
and folding Rachel's hands in hers,
prayed for her. It was probably
the first time in her life that Rachel
really knew what prayer meant, and
now she did not know clearly; she
had only a vague idea that some one
who was there, and she could not see
any more than if it was dark, was
sorry, and she was to be forgiven.
There stole into her heart a new feeling of regret, she did not know that
it was repentance, for as yet she had
not begun to realize how wrong a
thing an indulged temper is, though
she had often been told of it at the

Asylum. A bad temper is different from almost any other bad trait. It comes so suddenly, and is so overmastering, that those who have it are often made its victims, it would almost seem, without any choice on their part. If Rachel had known, when she felt herself swinging from the chair to the floor in Nancy's hands, that she was going to be angry, she probably would have tried to control it; but poor child, as I have said, she knew very little either what temper was or what control meant. While Mrs. Tilton was praying with her, for the first time an indistinct impression of having done wrong, or rather a heavy feeling about her heart, made her wish she could see Jesus, and go up to him and say, as Mrs. Tilton had, "Forgive me, I am very, very sorry."

She thought of him as she had seen
him on the great pictured cards
which her papa had brought her
from which to learn her Sabbath lesson, sitting under a tree surrounded
by a group of children, with his
hands on the heads of two. Her
mamma had told her he was blessing
them, and if he were only here, and
would put his hand on her, perhaps
he would bless her, and then that
would be the same as being forgiven,
for the children that were around
him looked so happy, as if none of
them felt sad and troubled as she did.

This was an important step for
Rachel. My readers will remember
what I said to them in the first chapter about the necessity of asking
Christ to forgive us and help us, if
we wish to conquer a fault, and that

we must be sincere and earnest if we expect him to do so. Rachel had at this time a feeling that there was somebody who must forgive her, and a desire to be forgiven. This was one step in the right way: repentance, and a desire to have the sin blotted out. So, when Mrs. Tilton asked her if she would not like to ask Jesus to pardon her, instead of standing, as she had at the Asylum, with only a dim, struggling wish, she fell again on her knees, and said,

"O, Jesus, if you se'ed me be very angry, and do all those naughty things mamma says I did, wont you make me never do so any more. Amen."

That was Rachel's first prayer; I mean the first one she ever prayed from her own heart in her own words.

Mrs. Tilton was reassured by its simple fervor ; and the hope that she had taken the right method in this first exhibition of Rachel's temper since she had adopted her, gave her courage for the future.

It was in vain that Nancy, whose good heart always very soon got the better of her impatience, now tried to blame herself more than Rachel, insisting that if she had had any sense, she might have seen as easy as not that little folks who never owned birds before wanted some time to love them in, without being plagued with sewing; that God made birds specially for them, and not squares of bed-quilts; and—and—in short, that dear little Rachel was about right, and she, old nurse Nancy, was growing too old, as this showed, to be trusted with the darlings any more.

It was in vain that Mrs. Tilton pointed to the wounds on her hands. She said they were "no more than pin-scratches, and not worth minding." So Mrs. Tilton was obliged. at

last, to insist that none of this too-
ready forgiveness should be shown
to the child, but that she should be
made to feel to the fullest extent the
wrong she had done.

When Nancy left Mrs. Tilton's
room, it was with a more imploring
look toward the cage than even Rachel's face had worn; but it was just
as unavailing. Mrs. Tilton only felt
that she had two children, an old and
a young one, to deal with, and must
be just so much the more firm. She
knew Nancy would gladly have carried it back, covered the child with
kisses, given her every pretty thing
she could find for her, and so make
friends again in the speediest manner
possible. Nor was she far from
right, as Nancy's behavior the moment she left her showed. Now it

must be known that Nancy, like a great many other good old women, had a fancy for marvelous cures, and was all the time concocting some astonishing kind of medicine. To do her justice she had been an uncommonly good nurse, and with her natural shrewdness had learned much of the proper treatment for sickness and suffering. Her sick friends often sent for her instead of a physician, and she no doubt helped the patient to be well quite as soon. Among her discoveries was a wonderful salve, which healed bruises, cured burns, closed cuts, took down inflammations, rubbed away swellings, removed sprains; indeed, it was equal, in its remedial effects, to the best quack medicine ever puffed in a newspaper. A box of this always stood on the table

by the head of Nancy's bed, and if
Mrs. Tilton had seen her, after she
left her room, she would have found
her rub the salve most energetic-
ally into every little mark which
Rachel had made, and then slide the
box into her pocket, to have it handy
for use any moment when she should
be alone. A stranger would have
thought Nancy the guilty one to
see the troubled look on her face as
she went toward the nursery; and
really the timid way in which she
turned the latch was very like that of
a naughty child, who does not know
what kind of a reception is waiting
within.

Rachel had got up from the floor
very soon after her mother had left
her, and had gone to the chair by the
window in which she had stood to

look at her birds. When Nancy
came in she found her there gazing at
the empty nail with such a sad,
troubled face, that in spite of her de-
termination to be very grave, and do
just as she knew Mrs. Tilton would
wish, Nancy could hardly refrain
from catching the child in her arms
and crying with and for her. As
it was, she tried to look straight
forward, as if she did not see her, and
walked up to the basket of patchwork,
with a fervent wish in her heart that
it was anywhere else, and made for
anything but Rachel's fingers.

"My dear," she said, and there was
a gentle tremor in her voice which
Rachel's ear immediately caught;
"My dear, it's a beautiful morning,
and mamma says when you have done
this pretty square you and I may go

and have a nice, pleasant walk on the
common. Come, darling, we will
have the red one you like so well,
and Nancy will thread your needle
and begin it for you all nice."

Rachel jumped down from the
chair and came to Nancy's side without any reply. The nurse ventured
a look at her. What a sad face it
was! so unlike her Rachel's. "Now
for the new thimble, the real silver
thimble, just like Nancy's, that mamma bought for you, and then the little finger; no, not the thumb, mamma
don't wear a thimble on her thumb ;
old Susan Price, whose fingers are all
stiff with rheumatism, does, but Rachel has eight fingers all made for
thimbles."

Rachel spread the whole eight
fingers before her. "Yes, I told you

so, dear little bits of fingers they are too. Nancy loves every one of them," and she put them to her mouth and gave them a kiss. "There, that will do. Now, here is the thimble finger; we will put the thimble on and then give it two more kisses to make it nimble, and sew little stitches."

Rachel held her hands still through all this, looking very steadily in Nancy's face.

The reader need hardly be told that the square selected was the prettiest in the basket, and that, when Nancy had threaded the needle and began it, she made it necessary to sew a long place before she handed it to Rachel, and then, when seated in her little chair at her feet the child had fairly commenced the task, she sat watching the progress of every stitch with a nervous impatience. which it was very well for Rachel not to see. After every few stitches Rachel raised her eyes toward the empty nail, and Nancy saw her lip quiver as she did so.

"O dear me!" she said to herself, "she'll burst out crying, and that will be the last of me; for certain as I live I shall catch her up and comfort her in spite of myself. I don't see how I can help it."

But she was mistaken; Rachel did not cry; she sat still and sewed, with her face growing every moment longer and sadder, so that, when she made a knot in her thread and broke it, Nancy was very grateful for the excuse for taking the work into her own hands and nearly completing what she had so kindly begun. Rachel's face did not brighten now as it generally did for any such help; it may be questioned whether she even felt as grateful for it as she should. There seemed to be but one thing of any interest to her, that was the empty nail from which the bird cage had swung.

Of course, the sewing was finished in a much shorter time than usual, and Nancy, delighted to have it over, hurried to dress Rachel and herself for their walk.

Rachel was generally a very pleasant companion; she saw and heard everything out of doors so quickly. It was, as Nancy often said to Mrs. Tilton, as good as a story in a child's story book to be with her; but to-day she did not seem to care for anything.

She went to her mother's room to say "good-by" before she went, and came back with tears in her eyes. Dick had seen her, and sung to her. Nancy wiped the tears away, and as she did so (O joy of joys!) Rachel took her wounded hand, covered with salve as it was, in her own, and kissing it, whispered,

"I am so sorry, O so very, very, very sorry; poor, dear hand, I wont ever do so again; never, never, never, never."

"Why, you blessed darling," said old Nancy, bending down to kiss her and dropping some big tears on the hands, "you didn't hurt me half so bad as it looks. There, now, we never'll do so any more, and then God will forgive us, and Nancy, she don't care nothing at all about it, only she

wants her darling to be a dear little
lady that Jesus can love. He don't
love any of your wicked, angry chil
dren. Didn't you know, when you are
angry, you are a city without walls?"

"What?" asked Rachel, whose ear
was always caught by anything new
and strange.

"A city without walls; haven't
you ever heard of it?" Rachel shook
her head, and when her hat was tied
on, and they were going down the
stairs hand in hand, asked again,

"What is a city without walls?"

Now Nancy was a good Bible
scholar, and knew more of the holy
book by heart than very many who are
younger and more intelligent. She
almost always had a verse ready to
quote on any important occasion, and
could generally explain its meaning

in her homely, quaint way; but for a
moment, to-day, she was puzzled, so
she said,

"Wait until we have had our
walk, and then I will tell you a little
story about it. This is the whole
verse, I will show it to you in my
big Bible when we come home:
'He that hath no rule over his own
spirit is like a city that is broken
down and without walls.'"

Rachel had already heard many
stories from that big Bible, and the
happiest hours of her day were when
Nancy had it in her lap, and was
talking to her; so she said, "When
we come home to-night, then we will
sit down and have a long story all
nice and good, wont we?"

"Yes, lamb, yes; so we will; and
now when we go out you can look all

around and see what a real city is, so
you will know the better." Nancy
was glad, if the truth must be told,
to have this time in which to think
up the story. Rachel asked so many
questions that it was difficult at any
time to answer her, and about this
city without walls, she did not feel
so sure herself. How could this little girl, who had no idea of cities, or
walls, or robbers, or enemies, or any
such things, be made to understand.
Well, the walk was to come now, and
the story by and by, so they went out.

It was a clear, bright December
day, such a day as hardly ever comes
to any city but Boston, where the
air is sharp, as if it was full of little icicles, and your hands and feet,
that you think you have hidden away
so nicely under warm coverings, are

found out and pinched and numbed, until you really begin to wonder whether you have not forgotten them, and left them at home.

Nancy's old blood did not move with quite so warmth-giving a flow as Rachel's, and before the walk was half over she was beginning to plan where she could stop to get warm, and find something that would be pretty and pleasing for Rachel. They had generally dropped into the bird fanciers in Court-street, but that would not do to-day. Never had the windows of the confectioners' shops looked so tempting before; but Mrs. Tilton, knowing how apt Nancy would be to make frequent visits to them if she found it pleasing to Rachel, had expressly forbidden it. The pictures in the windows were mostly of a kind not interesting to children, and there was no such thing as looking over children's books simply to gratify a child. While Nancy, with her ears and nose, her fingers and feet tingling with the frost, was in much trouble, wondering what she should do, the question was answered by a beautiful little white kitten's jumping into the window of a grocery which they were passing, and Rachel's noisy delight as she saw it.

To open the door and inquire if she could buy it was Nancy's first movement.

"Yes," the man replied. " It troubles me; it is so tame it is not afraid of any one, and is always under the customers' feet."

While they were talking, Rachel had caught the kitten, and sitting on

a box was hugging and kissing it, as
only little girls can, and looking so
radiantly happy, that, without a second thought, Nancy paid the man
what he asked for it, and told Rachel
it was hers, and she might carry it
home.

Even the shopkeeper and the
clerks stopped to watch her as she
danced around the store, fairly beside herself with delight; and kitty,
quite as happy to be loved as she
to love, purred and nestled down
close to her, and put her little vel-
vet paw all over Rachel's cheeks
without so much as showing that
she owned a claw, and turned her
white ears up and down, until she was
sure she had shown off their pretty
pink lining. Then she rubbed her
whiskers on Rachel's tiny muff to see

Rachel and her Kitten.

if it was not a mouse, and having satisfied herself with regard to all these
points, shut her green eyes and went
to sleep.

Not a thought besides the child's
enjoyment came into Nancy's mind,
until she saw that Miss Kitty was
likely to have a profound nap, and she
herself was thoroughly warmed; then
for the first time she remembered
Mrs. Tilton, and what she would think
of her purchase. It must be acknowledged that with the thought
many doubts occurred to Nancy, and
that the question of taking the kitten
home began to look not quite pleasant. She could carry it through the
streets under her cloak well enough,
if Rachel would let her take it. That
was not the point; but was not this
rewarding when Mrs. Tilton had pun-

7

ished? If she had a new pet, what was the use of the empty nail?

Ah, Nancy, good, kind old Nancy, you are not the only one whose wise judgment with children comes too late. Rachel would not suffer the kitten to leave her arms; she promised to hold her tightly, to cover her up warm, to protect her from any dog or boy they might meet. Nancy saw by the quick flash of her eye that it would not do then and there to press the matter, so leaving the rest of her walk unfinished, very reluctantly it must be confessed, she turned her face toward home. All the way she heard Rachel kissing the kitten, and the little thing at one time gave a most emphatic cry, as if the love had been a little too ardent for its comfort. " Now what will come?"

said Nancy to herself as they reached home at last. "Mrs. Tilton never makes half-way work with anything, and I am almost certain she wont thank me for this; perhaps I had better go right up first and settle it with her before Rachel has a chance to show it to her." This wise resolution she was prevented from carrying out by Rachel's pushing her away, and running up much faster than she could to her mother's door. Pushing it open, she rushed in with,

"O mamma! see, see what a dear, darling beauty she is!"

"What a cunning little thing!" said Mrs. Tilton, looking up from the book she was reading. "Whose is it?"

"My ounty tonty. Nancy said the man must give it to me, and he did."

Nancy by this time had come in at the door, and as Mrs. Tilton looked at her she saw in a moment that she was conscious of all the mischief she had done, so she only said,

"Nancy is very kind and good to you, Rachel; do you remember how you hurt her this morning?"

Rachel's face changed instantly, and, dropping the kitten, she ran to Nancy, caught her hand, and looking at it carefully, said,

"Must the kitty stay here too with the birdies? I will not cry. I will not be angry. I will try to be good."

"O, Mrs. Tilton, ma'am, if you had only seen and heard her," broke in Nancy; "before we went out you would have felt that she was repentant and never would do so again. It almost broke her heart to see how

she had hurt her poor, dear old
Nancy; and as for the kitten, why it
will always be a teaching her, a kind
of saying to her, 'now be gentle like,
and dön't you get angry.' You may
see by its very face, ma'am, that it's
all ready to say so to her." And
Nancy followed what she had said
with a series of expressive gestures
made behind Rachel's back.

Mrs. Tilton shook her head at her;
indeed, she was far from pleased, and
would gladly have sent the kitten
away, could she have done so without
further trouble. As it was she
said,

" Rachel, you may have her, and
take her to the nursery just so long
as you are well behaved; but the
first time you are angry I shall take
her away and shall not give her back

to you again, as I promised I would the birdies."

"When I am a city without walls will you take her?" asked Rachel. "Nancy says I was to-day, and to-night she is going to tell me what it means."

"Yes," said her mother, smiling, "when your walls are broken down, and whole armies of naughty, wicked feelings come rushing in, then kitty will be afraid to stay with such a child, she will want to run away somewhere else. No little pet loves a child that is not gentle, kind, and tender with it. Look in kitty's face; do you suppose she would shut her eyes and go to sleep so quietly if she thought you would be likely to strike or pinch her the next moment?"

Rachel held her kitten up and

kissed her, and as she did so, she looked so mild and loving that it was almost impossible to believe that she could be angry again.

"You may be right," said Mrs. Tilton to Nancy, "kitty may teach her what you and I cannot. Let us now hope for the best. She may play until time for her afternoon lessons, and then, Rachel, you must not object to kitty's being carried away until they are learned."

Dick sang very loud from his perch, and Nellie hopped down at this moment to dip its little bill into the water. Rachel forgot her new pet while she stood looking at them. O if she could only take them too, there would not be a happier child, she felt sure, in all the wide world. Nancy waited patiently for her until

the song was ended, then they went
to the nursery, where the first thing
Rachel's eyes sought was the empty
nail. She saw it for a moment only,
then the tears shut it out; nor could
the sight of kitty, now busily exploring the room, divert her from it.
That empty nail, how much it said
to Rachel! She sat down before it,
and fancied she saw the cage swinging from it; fancied she saw Dick
and Nellie; and then she listened
for the song; but she heard only
her conscience saying,

"Little girl, be careful, be very
careful to govern that bad temper of
yours. Ask God to help you."

CHAPTER V.

THE CITY WITHÓUT WALLS.

It was difficult for Nancy to restrain her admiration of the manner in which Rachel performed her afternoon tasks. Kitty was carried away without a word of objection, the long spelling lesson faultlessly learned, the wounded hands kissed so many times that no more salve was needed for their healing; and when the hour came, after tea, in which Rachel was accustomed to get the great Bible and read her evening portion over to Nancy, reciting her verse, and having, as a reward, a long story, it may be questioned which was the happier, the little girl or the old nurse.

Rachel would always draw Nancy's chair up before the bright grate, put her own close beside it, and then lay her head on the spotless white apron, which Nancy kept for "tending children in," and then the story was begun. To-night Rachel was not slow to claim the promise of the story about the city without walls; and as Nancy had profited by the hint conveyed in Mrs. Tilton's remark to Rachel, she was now all ready to begin, after reading with her the twenty-fifth chapter of Proverbs, which contained the verse.

"There was once a great, good King, who lived in a beautiful country far off from here. You don't know how beautiful the country was. Its rivers were waters of life, its seas were of glass, and its stones were precious stones; its houses were built of pure gold; its gates were pearls, and its gardens were full of flowers that never die."

"I should like to see those," said Rachel.

"Yes, darling, you don't know how pretty they are, and how happy all the children are who live there."

"Do they have birds and kitties?"

"They have everything they want to make them happy. Well, this great King has only those children live there with him who are good, and who have been tried. It is trial that helps people become good. Did you know it, Rachel?"

Now Rachel had a half-idea that a trial was something that everybody disliked, but must have, so she said "Yes," and Nancy went on. "But

as there is nothing in His country to
try them, He causes a child to
live first in another land, where she
will meet with a great many strange
and hard things. He lets her live
there, sometimes long years, until
she becomes old, and then, if all
these trials that she has met have
not conquered her, but she has conquered them, He takes her to His
land and makes her a child again,
and lets her stay there forever.
When He places her in this strange
land He builds a wall up around her
soul, which is the part that lives
with Him. It is just as if this soul
was a city, because there are so
many different things living in it.
There is what makes her smile
and what makes her cry, what
makes her love and what makes her

hate, what makes her happy and what makes her sorry, what makes her remember and what makes her forget, what makes her like pretty things and dislike ugly ones, what makes her want to do right and be afraid to do what is wrong, and what makes her very sad and troubled when she has done wrong; there is, too, the feeling that makes her want to pray and to read her Bible, and to like to hear about God and her Saviour. Now suppose every one of these things, and a great many more which I can't stop to tell you of now, were houses, don't you see what a little city full there would be?"

"A whole lot," said Rachel, "but what funny houses they are. Are they of gold too?"

"O no; it is only the houses in

that beautiful land where the King lives that are of gold."

"Is the child the soul?"

"Yes, they are the very same, only the child we see has a body that God has given to clothe the soul."

Rachel looked very much puzzled, but Nancy knew she could not make this clear, so she went on without observing it. "Well, around all these houses God builds a wall when he makes the child. It is a strange wall; outside it is very thin, and everything that comes against it could break it down easily if God hadn't put inside of it some curious kinds of gates, so that when the soul sees anything that will break the walls coming, if it is on the watch, all it has to do is to shut down the gates and everything within the city is safe;

nothing can then break the walls in, or tumble them down, or even get one single stone out from them. What is more curious still, no matter how little or how weak any little child is, it has the strength to shut these gates, even if it can't do anything else. Sometimes the king makes them so that if the child just wishes them shut they will close tight; and sometimes, when he thinks the child will be the better for it, he makes it very hard to close them, so that the owner has to tug and pull with all his might. Even then it occasionally happens that if he does his very best he can't move the gates, and the enemies from the outside break down the walls, and even the houses. Then he has to cry for help to the great King, who is always listening and ready, and comes right to the rescue, and with his own great hand closes the gates.

"This child that I was telling you about when I began my story came away from the beautiful home with its walls all strong and whole, and most of its houses filled with good people; but, and here is another strange thing, when the king makes this city he lets people who are not good get into some of the houses, evil ones, who are ready to help those who come from without, and destroy the child, so that it cannot go to the king's country."

"What does he do that for?" asked Rachel eagerly.

"Because he wants the child thoroughly tried, and it would be only half as hard to keep the enemies out from the outside if there were none within to help it. This child of whom I tell you we will call Zaidee."

"What a funny name!" said Rachel, much amused, and Nancy herself could not help laughing; but she had read it somewhere that day, and it was the first one she thought of.

"Zaidee's city had two bad enemies in it, but it was a long time before she found out anything about them. One enemy, who dwelt in a beautiful house, with everything as pretty and nice as could be, was Mr. Selfishness. Now Zaidee thought him a very pleasant gentleman, he had such winning ways, and he always had around him everything that anybody could want. Zaidee saw that he always had the best apples and pears and peaches and grapes, the prettiest

8

flowers, the prettiest pictures, and so many story books; but it took a great while to find out that what he had he kept, and that he also took away whatever he could lay his hands on that belonged to any one else. This was the way he kept constantly breaking down her walls. Zaidee had been placed in the care of a very good lady in the trial-land, and this lady had three other little children, all given to her by the same being. Now I will tell you just one instance of how Mr. Selfishness frequently served her:

"The lady had a fine garden, as good a one as often was seen in the trial-land, and she told the children she would give them each a little patch in it for a flower-garden, and who-ever should bring her the first and handsomest bunch of flowers from his own bed should have an elegant large picture book, which they all wanted. Well, most of the time the children were very happy together, and they laid out their grounds, and hoed and raked and planted their seeds, and enjoyed themselves. By and by the seeds came up, and then they weeded among them, and watered and watched them with a great deal of interest. Mr. Selfishness was very well satisfied, for Zaidee's garden looked just as well or a little better than any of the others for a long time; but Zaidee was indolent. After the newness of the thing had worn off, she began to be lazy about picking out every little weed, and if the sun had been hot, and they needed more than the pailful of water she had brought, she would throw herself down under the shadow of some tree and say to the others who were busy bringing their second pailful, 'How foolish you are! I dare say there will be a heavy dew to-night, and they will be as wet as sop. Come, sit down here with me, and hear that gold robin sing; there he is, on the pear-tree.' I rather think Mrs. Indolence, a fat widow, had oue of the houses in Zaidee's city, don't you?"

"Yes," said Rachel; "I would not let her stay; would you?"

"No; I should turn her out. She is almost as bad a tenant as Mr. Selfishness; and I can tell you, darling, you have no idea how often they live side by side. When you have had a flower-garden you will know that nothing very nice ever grows without care."

"When shall I have one ?"

"One of these days when we go to our home on Nelson's Island, and then you will see why the other's flowers grew taller and had larger buds on than any which Zaidee owned. Now Mr. Selfishness peeped out of his windows every day, and he began to grow more and more uneasy to see how fast the other flowers were outgrowing Zaidee's.

"'This will never do,' he said; 'we shall lose that book. We must contrive some way to make ours better, or theirs not so good,' and so he went to planning.

"He was the enemy within the city. Now the temptations were all to come from outside the walls.

There was the book, that was one; there was the flower-gardens all exposed, so Zaidee could injure them at any time she wished; there too was the love the other children had for Zaidee, never letting them suspect that she would or could do what would make them unhappy. These were the trials for her, or, as they proved, the enemies waiting to storm the gates; in other words, the opportunities given her for choosing what would make her fit to go and be happy with her King in the beautiful country, or what would shut her away from Him forever.

"So many plans as Mr. Selfishness made. But what do you think was the one which Zaidee chose? I am almost afraid to tell you, for fear you will think her such a naughty little

child you wont want to hear any
more about her."

"No, I shall not," said Rachel en-
couragingly.

"She got up early one morning,
very early, before the others were
awake, and went out into the garden
and picked off all the buds that were
larger than hers. There was a great
handful, so she did not at first
know what to do with them; and at
last, very much frightened for fear
they would be found, and she punished, what do you think she did?"

"I don't know," said Rachel.

"No more you don't, but I can tell
you. She went away off to another
part of the garden, dug a hole in the
ground, and buried them all there.
When the other children came out
to see how far their buds had opened

in the night, they found only the broken stems; nothing was left but the smallest and meanest flowers. Zaidee came with them, and tried to look innocent, and as if she felt very sorry; but she had to turn away and hide her face, it was so covered with blushes; she did not dare to have them look at her, for fear they would suspect her.

" Crying very hard, they all ran in to the kind lady under whose care they were, and she went with them to examine the garden. She noticed at once that none of Zaidee's flowers were touched, and although she had never known her to do such a thing before, she could not but think it very strange. So she called her, and asked her what it meant; and one wrong thing *always* leads to another.

Zaidee said what was not true. She said she had not been near them, and did not know anything about them.

" ' O, Zaidee, Zaidee, what a naughty little girl you are growing to be; how far you are wandering away from your beautiful home !'

" The kind lady looked at her very sorrowfully; she hardly knew what to say; and all the time Zaidee stood vexed and troubled, almost wishing she had let the flowers alone, but not quite, for she wanted the handsome book, which, she felt sure, must now he hers. Ponto, a great dog, with whom the children loved to play, came running into the garden, and, as if he knew there had something wrong been done, and they were unhappy, sniffed with his cold, yellow nose all around them; and perhaps he found out Zaidee was not good, for he pushed himself hard against her, as if he did not wish her to come too, then darted off before the others, calling them, as plain as a dog can speak, to come and have a play with him. They did not wait for a second invitation, but scampered with him, and away he dashed, down to the very part of the garden where Zaidee had hid the buds. Pretty soon he came upon her footsteps, and beginning to scent them, as dogs will, he followed them till he came to the little mound of fresh earth which she had piled up over the buds. This he soon turned over with his nose and paws; and there, not more than an hour after Zaidee thought they were gone forever, they

were all found, and the children
came back, bringing them in their
hands.

"Zaidee was so frightened that
she could not deny she had picked
them when the lady asked her.
But instead of being sorry, she
flew into a great rage, and struck
the children, then ran into their
gardens and began tearing up everything she could lay her hands
on.

"When the lady could stop her
she took her into the house, and shut
her up in a dark closet; and while
she was there, with nothing to do
and nobody to speak to, she began to
think about her city, and in what con-
dition its walls were. O dear, what a
place it was! It seemed to her as she
sat there, all alone in the dark, and

thought it over, that there was not a
single stone left one upon another,
but that the houses were all open
and exposed to whoever wanted to
come in. She found it very noisy
and busy there, and as she listened
she found how many wicked visitors
had stolen in through the gaps in the
wall, and the noise she heard was
their trying to take possession of
some of the good people's houses.
There was Miss Falsehood—what a
dreadful looking creature she was—
it made Zaidee frightened to look at
her. She strode in as soon as Zaidee
said she did not know who picked
the flowers, and was trying, with her
great bony hands, to pull Truth out of
her white marble house. But Truth
was asking the great King to let her
stay, and not give this wicked woman

room while there was any hope of Zaidee's wishing to repair the walls again and keep her out. There was Cunning, a very ugly boy, who picked his way pretty quickly through a crack in the walls, while Zaidee was stealing softly out of her bed in the morning, and looking all around, to be sure no one should see what she was going to do. He wanted to live in the house into which the great King had put Honesty; but the doors were tight locked yet, though the wall opposite the house was down. But Temper! Temper!" said Nancy, looking very significantly into Rachel's face as she said so, "Temper was the ugliest and the worst of all the wicked people that came in."

"How did he look?" asked Rachel.

"Look!" and Nancy was tempted to describe the way in which Rachel had looked and acted that morning, but she wisely forbore. "He looked monstrous ugly! His face was all covered with black and blue spots; he had one eye knocked in, his lips were as big as two great beets, and as for his nose, why, he had had it knocked so many times fighting, it seemed as if he hadn't any at all. I never saw such a sight in my life. Everybody got out of the way when he was coming; nobody ever likes to meet him for fear of being hurt."

"Did he have marks on his hands?" asked Rachel meekly.

"I rather think he did," answered Nancy with a smile; "there are always marks all over him, and it isn't likely his hands would escape. He went right to Sweet Temper's house, and he thundered away at the door as if he would knock it down; but the great king was there before him, and he dropped another bar over it; so thump and bang, loud as he might, he would never get in while the King staid there, and he would stay until Zaidee wore his patience out by having her walls tumble down too often. As for Mr. Selfishness, he began to be a little alarmed at what he had done; he only wanted the book; he did not want all these ugly people in the city, with the broken walls, and the angry King. No, indeed, these consequences had never entered into his thoughts.

"And that is always the way, Rachel. The wicked part of us that does wrong, in the end suffers more than the good part which it tries to injure, unless, indeed, we become all wicked, then all is lost together."

"Did the good King make new walls?"

"No; when the walls which he has built are broken down he leaves the city as it is, until by prayer and repentance, and trust in his Son, the child begins to lay one stone after another; then, when he finds she is in earnest, and really wishes to be safe within the gates, he helps her, but he only works just so far, and just so fast, as she is able and willing to work with him. You don't know, Rachel, how long it takes, and what hard work it is to build up again."

Rachel sat looking into the fire, evidently thinking intently over what she had heard. At last she asked:

" Where is Zaidee now ? Has she gone home ?"

" Zaidee ? O, Zaidee," said Nancy, puzzled; "why, Zaidee, she is only Rachel Tilton."

" Me !" said Rachel, " I never saw any great king, or any of those things you have been telling me about."

" Haven't you, my darling ? Well, heaven is the beautiful land, and God is the great king; he it was that made you and all the other little children that you see, and placed you here to be tried, so that you may grow to be good and pious, and when you die go to be like his blessed angels, and live in golden houses, and 'never have any need of the sun, for the Lamb is the light thereof.'"

Nancy said this very solemnly.

9

Rachel only half understood her, but she felt that it was true, and that there was something about her of which she had never thought before. After a few minutes' silence she asked:

"Are my city walls all broken down because I was angry this morning? Who lives there now?"

"Yes, Rachel, when you struck and pinched me, every blow went right against the walls, and you did not stop to shut the gates. O, I don't know what dreadful work they made, nor who has crept in to push the good people out of the houses. You will have to pray very often to God to help you, for his Son's sake, and work very diligently with your own hands to build them up again soon, and when they are whole and strong,

the wicked feelings do not stay.   God
shuts them out."

"And bars the gates?"

"Yes, but not so tight as to keep
them out, unless you are on the
watch.   When you find you are going to be angry be quick and shut
the gates."

"How?"

"Pray; say, 'God help me not to
be angry, for Christ's sake.   Amen.'"

"Will he help me?"

"Yes, always."

It was now Rachel's bed-time.
Nancy had told her of but one of
the wicked inclinations which within
her heart were ready to help the
temptations from without; but the
hands of the clock pointed to the
hour for bed, and Nancy well knew
how particular Mrs. Tilton was about

punctuality. So she put away her Bible, and Rachel, kneeling by her bed, prayed again. This time she asked God to make the walls of her city strong, to make the gates shut easily, to take away her naughty temper, and make her good.

My young readers, how is it with the walls of your city? Are they firm and whole? Is there no opening through which your "easily besetting sin" enters? When your great King comes down to visit you, will he find the streets all swept and garnished, the houses inhabited only by those whom he can approve?

CHAPTER VI.

THE CHILDREN'S MYSTERY.

OUR book would be too long should we follow Rachel through all the time which remains now between the night when Nancy told her the story of " Zaidee," and the place where we left her in our story about Ernest, when she had just come to Nelson's Island. We trust we have told our readers enough to make them acquainted with her, so they will feel interested in following her through the remaining volumes.

The winter passed very quickly and happily to her. When her new mother thought she had learned fully the lesson from the empty nail, she brought back the canaries, and it was many weeks before Rachel could look at them without being reminded of what had occurred on the morning of their removal. Kitty, too, whom she had christened Zaidee, for the little child who was going to the beautiful land, but always called "Zaid," was a well-mannered kitten, who ran for the ball or the string after the most approved kitten style, purred as loud as a happy kit need, slept long, long naps on the softest seat in the nursery, and never was known to attempt to kill the birds. Perhaps this was because they were entirely out of her reach; but whatever the true reason was, Rachel and Nancy thought it was because she was so very good, and gave her credit ac·cordingly.

Zaid always wore some kind of a ribbon or bead necklace around her neck, and was hardly allowed the usual privileges of kittenhood for fear some harm might come to her. During the winter she proved of much use to Rachel in the practical lessons her sweet temper taught, for she was never known to scratch, or bite, or even to insist on doing anything which her little mistress did not wish done. Rachel used to tell Nancy laughingly that "Zaid" had a city with walls all up, strong and even, and not so much as a loop-hole through which to peep out.

When the spring had passed, and the warm weather began to come, Mrs. Tilton was ready to make her usual removal to her cottage on Nelson's Island, and the reader already

knows of the surprise of Ernest and
Rachel upon meeting there. We
shall now take up our story from a
week after Rachel's arrival at her
sea-island home, by which time she
had become acquainted with Alice,
Tom, Sam, and Eddie, to say nothing
of the old wreck, the raft, and with
every other object of interest and
amusement.

No one can tell how delighted
Alice was to have a little girl-com-
panion. There was only one thing
which really troubled her: Rachel
seemed to prefer Ernest's company to
hers ; and even Ernest himself, though
he was her brother and not Rachel's,
loved to talk and play with Rachel
quite as well as with herself. The
walls about Rachel's city had become
much stronger than when Ernest last

saw her; or perhaps it would be better to say she had, through God's help,
learned to shut the gates more quickly. She was, at last, really beginning
to control her temper; but all this
we shall find out as our story goes
on.

One pleasant morning Sam knocked
very early at Mrs. Tilton's door.
Nancy had been up and out of doors
a long time. Zaid was there too; she
was always the last in the house to
go to bed, and the first to get up.
Nancy was weeding Rachel's garden;
she did not think it was quite proper
to do so when the child was around,
for fear it might teach her to depend
upon others; but if she had a chance,
when she thought she would not find
it out, you may be sure she was very
diligent about it.

Sam had come to tell Rachel that they were to go over, right after breakfast, to a small island, one mile from theirs, upon which they were going to do something great.

Now Sam was not a favorite with Nancy. He was too much of "a humbug." for that. So she got up, and, looking at him over her spectacles, said,

"So I suppose you think Mrs. Tilton is a going to let Rachel go off with you wherever you want to take her, without anything more, do you? I can tell you, you are very much mistaken."

"Tom is going too, and he sent me round to ask Rachel. He says we shall have prime fun."

"Don't feel sure," said Nancy, shaking her head. "Tom is a differ-

ent boy from Sam; but there aint
no telling. Anyhow, I shall run
over and see your mother about it
before I say a word to Rachel."

"Ernest is going, and Alice too."

"Who says so?"

"I say so," and Sam tried to look
very carelessly into Nancy's face; but
it would not do. Sam very well
knew his "say so" was not worth a
thought to any one, so he blushed
after all, and hung his head. That
was bad for Sam; but he was so
used to being distrusted, that more
than half the time he did not feel
quite sure whether he meant what
he thought he did himself.

"I mistrust you," said Nancy.
"Come, if your mother is up, I will
go home with you before Rachel has
any guess what is going on;" and

Nancy, without waiting for any reply, walked off toward Mrs. Cady's house.

She met Tom on the way with his arms full of pieces of old sail, rope, ends of home-spun carpet, and one old bed comforter. He tried to avoid her, but Nancy was not the kind so easily got rid of. She took a short path toward the spot where she saw that Tom would come out, and when he thought she must be almost to his mother's, where she frequently made an early call when there was any plan‑ for the children going on, she came suddenly upon him just round the pine-tree, and confronted him with,

"So you meant to get rid of me. Softly, my boy. The best way is to take old Nancy into your confidence, and tell her all about it to start with, 'cause, you see, Rachel can't go no other way in the world. Where are you going, and what are you going to do with all them old traps? La me, now, I wouldn't have them brought into our house on no account. There is no telling what an army of moths they have about them."

For a moment Tom hesitated. What splendid help Nancy would be, and how many things he should want that she could procure for him. He liked her too right well. To be sure, she scolded him roundly if she thought he was doing anything improper ; but when she approved, what a host she was." So now Tom looked very doubtfully up in her face.

"You'll tell," he said. "I never saw a woman who could keep a secret yet."

Nancy laughed a very good-natured laugh. There was something very droll to her in being spoken so to by a half-grown boy; but she said at the same time, "You are saucy, but that wont help you any. If you want Rachel Tilton, all you have got to do is to own up. She wont go a step a caracoling off with you boys on this mighty ocean, nobody knows where."

"You are not her mother," said Tom, trying to gain time for deciding what he had better do about the matter.

"No more I aint; but Mrs. Tilton never would let her go, no more than nothing, if I told her it wasn't safe. Try it, and see, if you don't believe it."

"I have half a mind to tell you; you could help us first-rate, and you would, I know you would."

"Try it, and see."

"Will you swear not to tell?" These words had slipped from Tom unawares. He did not mean to say what was wrong, and he was sorry the moment he had uttered them.

"'Swear not at all,'" was Nancy's instant reply, "'neither by heaven; for it is God's throne: nor by the earth; for it is his footstool; neither by Jerusalem; for it is the city of the great king. Neither shalt thou swear by thy head, because thou canst not make one hair white or black.'"

"Poh, nonsense, Nancy; you know I didn't mean any such swearing. I

should as soon think of asking a par-
son to do it. I only meant, say you
wont tell, certain true, black and
blue."

"Well, Thomas Cady, you are
making a great fuss about a very
little thing but if it's perfectly correct, and there ain't a jot of harm in
it any way, I'll use my judgment
about keeping it to myself."

"Can't go um," said Tom, swinging up the bundles, which he had
thrown down when first caught;
"you must keep the girl at home if
you have a mind to spoil a lot of
good fun for her, but I am too old
a salt to be caught sailing on that
sea."

Now, this alternative had not occurred to Nancy. Rachel had taken
so important a part in all the sports

of the children on the island that it
had not seemed possible to her that
ever Tom would think he could do
without her, so she watched him go
whistling away, expecting every moment to see him turn round and come
back, until he was almost out of hearing ; then she called after him, " Tom !
Tom ! I say."

Tom had been expecting this, but
he pretended not to hear, and walked
steadily on, so Nancy took a few
quick steps after him, and called
again.

"That's it," said Tom to himself,
" I shall have her on my own terms
soon." So he was deafer than ever,
but it all would not do. Nancy never
began what she did not mean to carry out, and not to hear her now
would have been quite impossible, so

at last he stopped, and turned slowly around.

" You calling me ?"

" I should think you ears had grown up. Where are you going, I say, and what are you after ?"

" Will you promise ?"

" No, I wont; I shall use my discretion about it."

"All one; good morning," and Tom lifted his cap with much politeness, and was going on again.

" Can't you stop a moment ?"

" No use. I am very busy ; got a lot to do. I am sorry Rachel can't come ; I quite counted on her, she is so spry and full of fun."

" Who says she can't ?"

" I thought you did."

" I only said I wouldn't promise to keep all your nonsense to myself."

" One and the same thing."

Nancy was beginning to feel warm; this was a kind of bantering to which she was not used. Tom could read faces pretty well for a boy, and he saw, as he looked back at her, that he had gone far enough, so he threw down his bundle again, and running to her said good-naturedly, " Come, Nancy, now you wont tell, will you? 'cause if you do you will spoil all our fun; and I should like to have you know, above all things, you could help us in so many ways. I am going to trust you, and if you are trusted, you know, it is ' honor true,' and you can't break over it any more than you can over a bounden promise any day."

"Trust me, then."

" Yes, I will, and if you peach, Nancy, I will never tell you a secret

again as long as my name is Thomas ·
Cady, nor will I take Rachel off on a
frolic this whole summer ; so there, I
have you."

Yes, he had, more firmly than he
knew. He drew Nancy behind a rock,
so that no one could see them from
the road, and sitting down, he seemed
to go very fully into these plans whatever they were, and to convince her
that nothing must be revealed to any
of the grown people on the island.
That Nancy did not think there
was anything very wrong in what he
told her we may judge from the
hearty laughs which came from her
every now and then, and the promise
which, after all, she did give in parting, that she would not tell any one
but Rachel, and that she would help
them all she could.

Sam waited for her a long time behind the corner of the woodshed. He had not walked to his mother's with her; she found so much fault with him that he was really afraid of her, so he had run home another way. Now he could not imagine what could have become of her. He was there still, watching and wondering, when Tom came back from depositing his "traps" upon the raft.

When Nancy reached home she found Rachel looking out of the window for her very impatiently. It was Nancy's business to dress her and read her verses in her Bible with her before she left her room, and now the sun and the birds had been calling Rachel, and she had been answering them for what seemed to her a very

long time. Rachel had to shut the
gates behind the city walls many
times while she waited. Impatient
Temper was knocking very loudly to
come in, but she kept all safe, and
though it was a flushed, eager face that
rushed to meet Nancy as she opened
the door, there was no more striking
or scratching. Rachel now had these
violent indications of her temper
quite under her control; and though
she sometimes felt as if it was impossible to stand or sit still when she
was boiling with anger, still she
found, in some mysterious way, that
it was never so hard to-day as it was
yesterday. One by one the upward
step now waiting to be taken is all
the more quickly and surely reached
because we have planted our feet
firmly on the round just below. Nancy

saw at a glance that Rachel's city was safe.

Before Rachel left her room Nancy had told her the secret; not, we would not have our readers think for a moment, in violation of her promise. No, indeed; Nancy was far too noble and true for that; but Tom had given her liberty not only to tell Rachel, but also to make some plans with her for carrying out his arrangements. Rachel was wild with delight; she danced and sang, whispered it to Dick, who came and put his head down to the wires of the cage to hear; caught up Zaid, and told it first into one ear and then into the other, and finally ended by looking very mysterious and happy all the morning when she was with her father and mother.

Nancy had asked leave for her to

be absent on a secret expedition all
day, and Mrs. Tilton had readily
granted it, as she knew if Nancy approved all was safe and right. She
had a hint given to her, too, that if
she would neither seem to see or
hear, it would add a great deal to
the children's happiness; so she was
very kindly deaf and blind to everything that went on around, and
when Ernest and Alice came running
up to the door for Rachel she was
all ready, with a great covered basket, half as large as herself. The
children walked very demurely so
long as they were in sight of the
windows of the house, only talking
with those looks and signs so intelli-
gible among themselves; but the very
moment they were hidden down went
the basket, and they danced round

ıt more like a set of Indian warriors
than anything else. Alice wanted to
lift the cover and peep in, but this
Rachel shook her head over, saying
with much authority:

"Wait! wait! it will be soon
enough when we get there." ·

"But my mother didn't give me
half so much. I will show you. Ernest hid it in the ship, so no one need
suspect. It is only a tiny tin pailful,
so large," and Alice's hands measured
a supposed pail of all sizes, from three
inches up to a foot.

" O Alice! you know it has lots of
nice things in. I saw them myself,"
said Ernest.

"Hush! don't tell," and Alice
raised her finger at him. "Let's run
for it first ;" so Ernest, taking hold of
one side of Rachel's basket, the three

children were soon on the old wreck.
Rachel could run up the ladder at the
sides quite as nimbly as the boys, and
by this time she had begun to feel as
if it was her property as much as
theirs. She had carried some of her
prettiest playthings there, and very
often, on a warm summer morning,
the canaries were brought down, and
added a great deal to its pleasantness
with their sweet songs.

This morning the boys from Uncle
Seth's were there before them. Tom
had been making his plans for a long
time, and, good general that he was,
did not mean, when the occasion
came, to be found wanting in any of
the necessary supplies. So ever since
breakfast Sam and Eddy had been
busy transporting hidden stores from
their places to the wreck. Here

Loading the Raft.

came an old three-legged chair, almost as good as new since the wanting leg was supplied with a round billet of wood; then a small table, with only one original support left, but fixed upon a curiously shaped block, which had been washed up, and stood quite firmly if well propped; but we must not anticipate.

Busy children are always happy, and almost always good. It is only for idle hands that Satan finds the "mischief still;" so you may be sure that these very busy children were also both happy and good. Everybody was so willing and obliging, that long before they had thought it possible to be ready they were formed into a procession, and were marching down with their odd property toward the raft, which lay hauled up high and dry on the shore. This raft was now a very nice bit of sea-craft. The sailors who saw it pronounced it a much safer thing for the children to venture out upon the water in than any boat, and they had been so in the habit of going and returning safely, that their parents had lost all fear of accident if Tom were there to act as helmsman. It was carefully stored with as many of their commodities as it could well carry, and then came the question, which of the children should go over with Tom first? Of course, every one was eager to go ; and here, at the very beginning, trouble would have come, if Tom had not insisted on his rights as captain to make his choice. He chose Ernest and Rachel, and, deaf to all complaints from the others, rowed away.

CHAPTER VII.

HOW THE STRENGTH OF RACHEL'S WALLS IS TRIED.

THE sea upon which the raft was sailing was delightfully smooth, and so blue and deep that it made Rachel think at once of that beautiful land to which Nancy had told her Zaidee was going. She looked down, and it seemed to her that it was a sea of glass, and that beneath it were the precious stones and the houses of gold and the gates of pearl. She remembered, too, what was better than this, that Nancy had said that she was one of the children the King had placed in the trial-land, and she resolved that all the time they were

about this pleasant play she would
try and keep her city walls whole,
and have her gates ready to move
quickly on their hinges and shut her
in.   These thoughts did not stay
long in Rachel's mind; but I need not
say God sent them; we all know
that.

They went direct, wind and waves
aiding, to a very little island one
short mile from the point where they
had started. This island, from being
so pretty and so small, had always
been called the " Children's Island,"
and they felt as if it belonged to
them as much as the old wreck of
the old ship. It was nothing more
than a large rock, upon which the
winds and the waves had dropped
soil and seeds, until trees and shrubs
had come up and made it quite a

shaded spot. The children knew
every inch of it, and could tell which
was the largest pine-tree, where the
scrub-oaks grew nearest the ground,
and where, by some odd freak, the
wintergreen berries ripened quickest
and sweetest. They had their port
here and their wharf, and now they
had come to take legal possession and
make formal settlement. The secret—
it will out, so we may as well take our
readers into our confidence at once—
was to build a sort of Robinson
Crusoe house, have their church, their
school-house, their stores ; in short, be
all ready when Captain Lee returned
(he was expected back at the end of
August) to give a party for him, and
entertain him, as Tom said, "like a
prince." No one of the older members of the families were to be admitted

into the secret; it was to be a surprise to all. Now any one can see
that so extensive a plan as this among
six young children would put them
all into positions and circumstances
that would greatly test their character; and so the events proved.

Ernest had learned to pull an oar
very well for so small a boy, and he
was so much help to Tom that in a
short time they touched the wharf,
and with many formalities Tom
sprang on shore, ran up to the top
of the rock, and swung out the stars
and stripes from a pole put up for the
occasion. The children on Nelson's
Island saw it and shouted impatiently. There wasn't one of them but
would have walked over the water
to it if they could.

Eager children work quickly, and

very soon the raft was cleared, and
Tom was once more crossing the water. He wanted to bring over a load
before he took what he called his
"live stock," but the children would
not hear of it, and with his usual
good-nature he carried them first.

Ernest and Rachel had been busy
in the mean time selecting a spot for
their house. They played that they
were an emigrant ship, wrecked, and
all on board lost but one man
(Tom) and five children. While
the man had gone to the wreck to
bring off the rest of the saved, it
was their business, with all haste, to
provide the home.

Now about this home there had
been a variety of opinions expressed
before they started, some wanting
one spot chosen, and some another;

but the last thing Tom had said was
that Rachel might choose, and the
others should abide by her decision.
So, now, Ernest and Rachel were
busy exploring, and feeling very wise
and important.

After a thorough search, they decided upon two places. One, where
the main rock upon which the island
was founded ran up to a point, and
just below this point, upon which the
flag was flying, another rock met it,
forming a snug sort of a room. It
was nothing like a cave ; it was rather
a large hollow, quite large enough to
hold the six children at once, besides
a table, and perhaps a chair. This,
then, for the beginning, and for one
side of the real house they were in-
tending to build. The other place
had in it this morning what children

all love so well, bright sunshine. It was a spot between four pine-trees, all nearly the same shape and size, with their broad arms meeting above and making a roof. All over the ground, so smooth and slippery from the dead leaves of the trees, the sunlight lay in patches; beautifully checkered it was, almost as if some fairy had begun to pave it with gold. And then they could see Nelson's Island from the front door, a very desirable thing to poor shipwrecked, homesick mariners. So Rachel decided that this should be the spot, and Ernest, very well pleased, began to drag thither the articles from the wharf. By the time the raft had returned almost everything had disappeared from the landing-place, and when Alice came she found Rachel quite taking upon herself airs as mistress of the house.

Alice had been, as we know, without any one to share her pleasures until Ernest came, and we must not blame her too much if she often thought her own way the best, and that everybody else should follow it. She was not naturally more selfish than most other children, but she had never been obliged to give up to the wishes of others, excepting when she played with her boy cousins, and then if she was displeased she always took refuge in running home to her mother. Since Ernest had been with her she loved him so much, and he was so gentle and yielding, that she was not really, in these particulars, gaining so much from her little new brother as her parents had hoped.

But her mother was very watchful,
never allowing this fault of hers to
pass under her notice unreproved.
Since Rachel had been on the island
she had been obliged to see a rival
coming in to do many things which
had been her sole right before.
Sometimes she bore it pleasantly,
and sometimes she sulked, and they
could not make her join in the play
again without a great deal of teasing.

Now two things displeased her.
One, that Rachel should have been
brought over first, when she wanted
to go; and another, that she should
have been allowed, without her voice,
to choose the home. We must say
we do not think this was quite fair
in Tom. It would have been better,
and more in American style, if they
had all come together and chosen their

several shares in the performances by
acclamation or by vote, or in some
such impartial way. Still Alice's
mother had always taught her that it
was very mean for one child to spoil
the fun of all the others because she
was not satisfied, and Alice had begun
to think of it as almost a sin to be
cross and sulky for such a cause.
But how many of us there are who
determine not to do this, that, and
the other wrong thing, but when we
are tempted cannot resist, and fall
very easy victims. So it was with
Alice to-day. That very morning,
when she said her prayers, she had
asked God to make her a good, pleasant little girl all day long, to keep
her from being selfish, or cross, or
sulky. There was one thing her
father had often told both Ernest and

herself for which they should never forget to pray, and this Alice remembered particularly; it was, that God would make them generous and noble in their plays, would make them kind and unselfish with their young friends, and give them the love of other children.

There are many children who are taught to pray properly who still remember only their relations to God in their prayers. They think that they are to pray for the salvation of their soul so that they may go to heaven. That is right; but they should also pray that they may be happy, and have a good influence here that may make others happy, and love and be loved. This is an important part of our preparations for that beautiful land. Alice was

earnest in her intention to remember
all this when she left her room that
morning; but how soon we forget.

When Tom landed the second time,
he applauded the young workers very
heartily for what they had done.
He said the "house lot couldn't be
beat," and the shelving rocks were
meant for a store-house and nothing
more; and even the little cloud, which
was settling down over Alice, was
lifted up by a sight of the cunning
place which was to hold the "ten-
ement." Two loads more of old
boards and material needed for building were to be brought, and Tom, taking first Ernest and then Sam, went
over to bring them. While they
were gone Alice and Rachel began to
plan out the interior of the house,
dividing it into parlor, kitchen, and

dining-room, and one sleeping-room. Now Rachel wanted the parlor arranged first, and Alice the kitchen; so they had a little dispute about it, not a very bad one, but enough to throw a slight shadow over the bright spots of sunshine on the tesselated ground, and it ended in Alice's beginning the kitchen with Eddie to help her, while Rachel had Sam or Ernest, whichever was not on the raft. This would have done very well, for in case of dispute separation is always the wisest course; but they were both so often wishing the same thing that they came into constant collision. Once Rachel grew so angry, to see Alice snatch away a bit of old carpet from Sam, saying that it must answer for a mat before the kitchen door, while she wanted it before the parlor fireplace, that she flew at her, pulled the carpet away, and shook her roughly. So when Tom came up from the raft with the last load he found Alice sitting at quite a distance from the house crying, and Rachel, with a flushed and downcast looking face, moping about the house as if she had lost every friend on earth.

"Hey dey!" he said, stopping abruptly; "what is to pay now? There is always trouble in the camp when there are women around. Ally, what's the matter?"

"She shook me," said Ally, lifting her face, all covered with tears, and pointing to Rachel. "I don't like her one bit; I wish she had never come here."

"That's not polite, Miss Lee. We emigrants can't quarrel among our-

selves; if we do there will be mischief to pay. There may be savages
here, who knows?"

. Rachel thought at once of her city
walls, and how badly they were
broken down, all ready for the savages
ages to enter; but she was not peni-
tent enough to care now.

"Come," said Tom good-naturedly,
"own up, Rachel, what did you shake
Alice for? We are not shaking
Quakers here."

"She took it, and would keep
snatching it away from Sam. It's for
the parlor, and not for the kitchen
mat, and she sha'n't snatch it."

"What! is it that old bit of carpet
you are quarreling over? Well, here
goes," and taking it up, Tom threw it
as far as he could over the water. It
spread itself out and floated for a

moment on the top of a wave, and
then slowly sank away from their
sight. Both children forgot everything else in watching it, and Tom
always afterward called this his
"masterstroke of discipline." "So I
shall end all disputes," said he, when
it was fairly gone. "Whatever anybody quarrels about both shall lose,
and we shall all lose it too, so I think
the better tempers we can keep, all
hands of us, the better for our new
settlement. Halloo, now, no more
playing; all hands to work in earnest.
The first thing to be done is to build
the house, and then we will furnish it
as best we can. Here, Alice, hold
this box of nails ready for me the
minute I want it. Now, Rachel, go
with Ernest, and drag round that
pole ; it must be nailed across from

tree to tree to form the ridge-pole of the house. Sam, find the next longest, and don't be two minutes having it here; and, Ed, you pick up bits of dry wood ready for the fire, by which we are going to cook our dinner. We must get a house built first for fear of intruders, and then we will be ready for a bite."

Sam had already helped himself out of Rachel's basket in a private way; he never saw the time when he would not "eat on the sly," as Tom said, if he could get a chance. Alice's tears were dry. She felt a great deal happier than Rachel, when she went to work, for Rachel was more conscious of having done wrong.

Before dinner-time came quite a house was built. To be sure, they had not plank enough to make the

walls very close, but that was not
necessary; and as for shutting the sun
out with a roof, who would think of
it for a moment? Old sails and the
comforter made the inside partition;
and when the fire was kindled in the
rude fireplace, (which was mostly com-
posed of oyster-shells,) and a fish,
caught late the night before, was laid
upon an old gridiron to broil, there
was not a happier set of children in
the world. Wonderfully happy they
were, considering the loneliness of
their position, and the disputes with
which they had begun the day.

Now came Nancy's share in the
enterprise. When Rachel's large
basket was unpacked, what a treasure
of good things it contained! The
fish was "done to a turn," Tom said;
and though an experienced cook

The Picnic on the Island.

might, perhaps, have thought one part a little too much blackened, and the other not quite done, still never was feast so delicious as this. The dining-room, with the sun shimmering in between the long needle-like leaves of the pine-tree, and laying itself like a service of gold all over the odd table; the soft summer breeze, filled with life and vigor as it came to them over the sparkling water; the low song, which the waves sang for them, and in whose chorus every child's heart joined; the birds alighting on the old limbs above their heads, and peeping in with their round brown eyes to see what the little folks were doing, and their own good-natured prattle; certainly fewer things than these have made children happy. For a time nothing could exceed their enjoyment. If there had been any moments during the morning when they were questioned whether their hard work "would pay," they were answered now. But, somehow, it seems to be always when we are happiest, and least on our guard, that our temptation comes. Among Nancy's stores was a nice supply of raisins. These, with the greatest impartiality, Rachel had counted out, laying an equal share by each plate, or rather by every bit of china which served for a plate. Sam and Ernest sat side by side, and it was not very long before Sam's sly ways began to show themselves in his taking one raisin after another from Ernest's heap, while all the time he would have his head turned another way, and be talking very busily about something

in which Ernest was interested.   This
had not been going on long before
Rachel spied him, and the first knowledge he had of the detection was so
smart a blow upon his cheek, that
for a moment he hardly knew where
he was.   Sam's temper was very
quick too, and in another instant
he had sprung upon Rachel, and she
would have received such a speedy
and severe punishment for her offense
as had never been hers before if Tom
had not seized the children and held
them apart.

"Hands off!" he said promptly,
"what is all this row about?   Rachel, what did you strike him for?"
And the big boy's grasp was very
tight on Rachel's arm.

"He was stealing Ernest's raisins,"
said Rachel, struggling to get away.

12

"Well, what if he was? That was my business, not yours. The next time you lift your hand to strike a blow you shall be put on board that raft and taken home before you can say Jack Robinson. Do you hear me?"

"Yes," said Rachel, yielding at once to the "powers that be."

"Well, then look out; we don't allow fighting in any shape, getting mad, lying, stealing, or breaking any other of the ten commandments in our colony. The punishment in any case is instant exile." Before he had finished this long speech there was a good deal of drollery in Tom's face, which rather took away from his authority. So Sam began to rub his cheek and act as if he meant to make fun of the whole thing; but he had "mistaken his man," as Tom said, this time.

"For you," he said, dropping Rachel's arm gently and taking Sam by both arms, in the manner of an arresting officer, "I arrest you for stealing and fighting, and condemn you to banishment from our house and work for the remainder of the afternoon. In case of any resistance or trouble on your part I shall increase your punishment as it may seem best to me, the governor, in whom is vested all legal authority. Now go, sir; I confiscate the rest of your dinner, and drum you out of camp." So saying, Tom took up an old tin pail, which had come over to act the part of a bell, and pushing Sam out to quite a distance beyond the pine-trees, stood beating with a stick upon the pail in a very noisy, provoking way.

Sam was by no means content to go without a struggle. He tried to kick and snatch the pail away, and failing in that, he kicked and struck Tom, behaving as only a very naughty, angry child can. But Tom was so much the stronger that it was of no use. Sam had to take to flight, and content himself with firing back stones from such a distance as made this occupation safe.

The children returned to their dinner after he had gone, but the pleasure of the whole thing was gone too. They ate what remained in silence, or in discussing what a very naughty boy Sam was. It was in vain that the sun and the ocean, the summer air and the birds tried to make them happy. If Rachel had only shut the gates of her city soon enough, such a host of unhappy feelings would not now have been marching in over her broken walls, and Sam would not have been sitting, silent, sullen, and angry, out on the rock behind the house, wishing a great many things which would not have entered into his heart if his city walls had not been so rudely assaulted. Not that we mean to defend Sam's meanness and selfishness; far from it; but we want to impress it upon our young readers how often a gap in their own city walls leads to large rents and fissures in the walls of neighboring cities.

CHAPTER VIII.

SAM'S PUNISHMENT.

IT was in vain, after these events, that the children tried to get back the fun and interest which had made their morning so happy. Sam hovered, like a discontented spirit, within sight of them, but never came near enough to need to be sent away again. Occasionally he would dart down and take away an article which he saw them about to need in their work, giving Tom a chase, and making him say some quick, harsh words, for which he felt immediately sorry; and sometimes Sam threw a stick of wood, or a stone with good aim, knocking down some part of the

building which they had erected.
But this was by no means the worst
part of his behavior. He looked so
sullen that all the sunshine in the
world could not make the others happy with that face near them. Rachel, too, had lost the merry good-
nature which added so much to their
enjoyment. She knew she had done
wrong, and she was sorry. Now, if
being sorry would only do away the
past, how well it would be for us ; or,
perhaps, not so well after all, for
God has ordered these things just as
they shall work out for us our present and eternal good ; and he knows
that if feeling regret could do away
a sin, we should none of us be half
so careful to abstain from evil. It is
the dread of consequences not to
be remedied, that he has given

as a warning to keep us from doing wrong.

Rachel would have done anything in her power to have Sam back with them, to hear his happy laugh, and see his handy, helpful ways; but nothing that she could do would avail, and she missed him so much. If it had been a case where she had not been the first offender, she would have begged Tom to let him return; but now she did not dare to; and Tom answered so savagely when Ernest asked for him, that it took away what little courage she had.

In truth Sam, by his continued attacks upon the camp, was preventing any leniency which Tom might have been inclined to show. The afternoon, under such circumstances, would, of course, be long and rather dull;

the life and spirit of the whole thing had died out, and if we must confess what we think to be the real reason, we should be obliged to say that it was because Rachel had not kept her city walls. Twice, to-day, they had been invaded and had fallen.

By the time the sun began to go down toward the western sea the children were thinking often of home, and wishing they were there. Yet they looked with a great deal of pride and pleasure upon their day's work. It was a very pretty spot; any one would have known that children's hands had built it. It looked like a big baby-house, much more than like the home of shipwrecked mariners, but that was just as well; it was right pleasant and taking, what more could they ask.

Alice was the first one to express a wish to go home. She had not been quite comfortable since her shaking in the morning, though she had tried many times during the day to be generous, unselfish, and to make the others happy, as she had asked God to help her to do in the morning. Alice, you see, knew that prayer, true prayer, is not only asking sincerely, but trying to carry out what you have asked for. She was made still more uneasy by Rachel's quarrel with Sam, and now, tired and homesick, she began to long for her home and her mother, with a desire far greater than that of finishing the school-house upon which they were busy.

"Yes," said Tom, when Eddy joined with her; "yes, yes, I am as tired as a whipped dog. I tell you what,

Ernest, if this is play I don't know
what work is. I have heard Uncle
William say, when I have been building some of what he calls my air-castles,
about being captain one day of the
handsomest ship of the line that ever
sailed from Boston harbor, ' Uneasy
lies the head that wears a crown,'
and if every governor has such a tug
as I have had to-day, here is one fellow who wont run for 'the chief
honor in his state' for some years
yet, I can tell you. Come, we will
make snug, and be off in fifteen minutes. All hands, ahoy! Man the
ship. Spread the sails. Hoist the
anchor. Three cheers for port."

With scarcely less enthusiasm than
they had shown in the " dew of the
morning," the children were now
busy putting up things in such a

way that no intruders should do them harm during their night's absence, for they were to return early in the morning. They had many a day's work before them yet to make the necessary preparations for the grand party.

While they were thus occupied, Sam, who had become very restless, from being so long shut out by himself, came near where they were, to put in execution his final piece of mischief. He had determined to creep in at the kitchen-door and tear down the partitions, throwing them in a heap in the middle of the parlor, where they should astonish the others on their return to-morrow, and make them think some persons with evil intent had been on the island. This he succeeded in accom-

plishing unseen. The partitions were
not firmly fixed, and they yielded easily. Laughing with much revengeful enjoyment over what he had done,
he came down boldly to the wharf,
to sail with the others for home.
But, unfortunately, Tom had returned for a moment to the house, and
seeing the mischief which had been
done, knew at once who was its au-
thor; so, without saying a word, he
went back to the raft, saw one child
after another seated upon it, and
whenever Sam tried to go he held
him back. When all were on board
he sprang quickly on himself, and as
he pushed off, leaving Sam standing surprised on the wharf, he called
out,

"We shall leave you here, sir,
until to-morrow; you will have the

whole night to put those partitions back; and 'I advise you to go to work and do as much as you can before dark."

Everybody thought Tom was in fun, and the children laughed at the joke of being left, to which in one way and another they were all accustomed; but Sam had a slight feeling of fear mingling with his sense of the fun.

How quick Tom had found him out, and how determined he looked at him from under his cap. Still, Sam made his mind up not to take the thing seriously; so he waved his cap back to them, and wished them good-night, with as great an appearance of unconcern as he could.*

There he stood, the raft leaving

* See Frontispiece.

more and more blue water between
them every moment; how blue and
deep it was. Sam looked down into
it, earnestly wishing he could run
over it and catch the raft before it
was any further away. On it went,
until it seemed like a speck on the
waters. Once in a while he could
Ernest would stand up and wave
his cap, and Sam always waved his
in return, but he saw no sign of
their turning around. The white sail
curved charmingly in the evening.
breeze; but it was filled toward home,
and thither, too, the rudder unswerv-
ingly steered.

"When are you going back?" said
Ernest at last, thinking the joke had
been carried far enough.

"To-morrow morning," replied
Tom.

The children all laughed, and the raft danced on.

"I say, Tom, don't keep Sam waiting there any longer; you will get us all late home, and mother will be anxious about Ally," said Ernest again.

"Have you there in ten minutes, or less."

"Why, no, you can't, it will take that time to tack her round, and bring her along side Sam."

"Sam will stay some time before the raft comes along side of him."

"You don't mean, Tom," said Alice eagerly, "that you are going to leave Sam there alone on that island all night?"

"I mean that I shall not take this raft across again to-night, and that, if Sam has all night to learn to mend in, he probably will have his lesson well committed by to-morrow morning."

"That aint fair," said Alice.

"Who says it isn't fair?" said Tom, lowering down upon her.

"I say so; don't you too, Rachel?"

"I do," said Ernest, without waiting for Rachel to answer; "and if I was only a little bigger I would go over to the island myself and bring him home."

"If is a great word," said Tom scornfully. "Little Hop-o'-my-thumb needn't brag."

"You are mean," said Rachel, breaking in.

"You don't say so. Well, now, do tell!" and Tom's voice was very provoking.

"You are, too," shouted Eddy

13

"and I will tell mother the very moment I get home."

" Go it, young one ; do you want a
ducking ?" and Tom held his hands
toward Eddy, as if he meant to throw
him in, so Eddy shrank close to Ernest's side.

" Let him alone," said Ernest in a
manly way. " Look here, Mr. Tom,
you think, because you are big, you
can do as you have a mind to ; but I
think it is very mean in you, as Rachel says, to be bullying little fellows
so, and when I grow larger I will
settle with you for it, you see if I
don't."

Tom laughed again ; but in his
heart he was too good-natured to like
to have the others all against him. He
was vexed with Sam, and doubtful as
to the brotherly character of the act

of leaving him alone. There is never a time when we can bear so little from others as when we are not sure of ourselves. They were now half way between the island and home, and Tom had for a moment some idea of taking the whole party off to Egg Island or the Light-house as a punishment. But we must do him the justice to say that this thought was but momentary, and that his better nature triumphed quickly, so he set his teeth tight together, (a way of doing that he had when he wanted to control himself,) and with a few strong strokes of the oars sent the raft rapidly toward home.

Eddy began to cry, so did Alice; but it was of no use, the raft touched the shore. Tom sprang off, fastened it, and without speaking a word to any one went away by himself, but not toward home.

"I say it's a shame; I'll go right home to mother."

"And so will I," sobbed Eddy; "she will make him go back quick, you see if she don't, double meter, I can tell *you*." And little Eddy, under the wing of his mother's authority, seemed to himself to have suddenly grown quite large.

"And my mother will say it's awful cruel in him; and there is poor Sam all alone, frightened most to death, I know he is;" and Alice cried harder than ever.

Ernest had not left the raft; he stood by it wondering if he would not be able to loosen and take it over himself for Sam; but his mother had expressly forbidden his venturing up-

on the water alone until he became
older, and when he remembered this
he knew it was useless for him to ask
permission.

Rachel would have seemed, to any
one who did not know her, almost
unconcerned about what had taken
place; but those who did know her
could have seen, from the flash of her
eyes, and her tight suppressed lips,
that she was trying to keep down her
temper, to shut the gates while there
was time. Perhaps she was helped
in all this by the feeling which there
was at the bottom of her heart that
she had been the occasion of all the
trouble. Poor Rachel has many hard
lessons to learn, but in after life she
looked back to this, in which she had
made so many persons unhappy, as
one of the very hardest of them all.

She did not like to go home. To tell her mother that Sam was left would be to confess all that she had done. She would get no pity from Nancy; indeed, she dreaded the shake of her head, and the blame she would receive from her, more than anything she expected from her mother. What could be done? who would help her?

The other children, thinking more of Sam than of her trouble, left her standing, looking out over the sea with a very sad face. So she found herself alone, with only that dismal, dismal moaning that the ocean made as it broke upon the shore. Rachel here, and Sam on the island, were at the same moment listening to it, and with feelings not dissimilar. Sam had not believed that they would really leave him until the raft was fairly out of sight; then he began to call, louder and louder, as there was less probability of his receiving an answer, until, frightened by the sound of his own voice, he stopped, looked around him timidly, and at last began to cry. With the first burst of tears all his angry, sullen feelings left him, and fear and loneliness gradually took entire possession of him. By the time the raft had reached home, and the children had landed, Sam would have been willing to say anything in the way of promise for the future, or amendment for the past, if it had been possible; but, alas! it was now too late. It was yet broad daylight, or the rays of the sun were only beginning to fade, still Sam was very conscious of every change in the light. The dark pines looked darker; they

sang from under their boughs a louder, sadder song, and the ocean, how it
did moan, moan, moan!

It is never pleasant to hear of a
frightened child, so we will leave
Sam standing there, screaming and
crying by turns, calling in vain,

"Tom! Tom! Tom! if you will
only come back for me I never will
do so again."

While Rachel at last goes sorrowfully home, Eddy finds his mother
and tells her; but she only regards it
as one of Tom's tricks, and thinks he
is already on his way to bring Sam
back, so she does not trouble herself
about it.   Alice and Ernest meet
their mother coming for them, and
though she thinks Tom too arbitrary,
still she blames Rachel, and hopes a
hard lesson will do Sam good.   She,

too, thinks Tom has gone back, and expects every moment to hear the boys' voices as they come walking past her house together. So Alice and Ernest are comforted, and after a hearty supper, and a pleasant evening talk with their dear mother, they go to bed and forget poor desolate Sam. Not so Rachel, though of her experience we must tell in another chapter.

CHAPTER IX.

RACHEL'S REPENTANCE.

IT was so late when Rachel opened the front gate that she found Nancy standing on the door steps waiting for her, and her mother called as soon as she heard her, to know if anything had happened.

Rachel hardly knew what answer to make; she knew her mother meant to inquire if there had been any accident. There certainly had not, but still there was so much wrong that Nancy noticed the hesitation in her "No, mamma," and determined "to go to the bottom of the matter" before she allowed Rachel to go to sleep. Now, therefore, she

petted the child in her usual way,
gave her the delicacies which she had
been keeping for her supper, and was
so kind and gentle with her that Rachel could hardly keep from bursting
into tears several times. Nancy noticed all these marks of emotion,
and felt the more confirmed in her
opinion.

As it grew dusk, a child came
running in from one of the fisher-
men's huts to say that his mother was
very sick and wanted Nancy, whose
knowledge of medicine made her in
great request among the poor people
on the island. Nancy forgot everything else in her kind desire to take
with her all that might be needed,
and hurried away, entirely forgetting
her doubts of Rachel.

Rachel watched her until she was

out of sight, and then very quickly
resolved to do what she had wished,
but had hitherto no idea of being
able to perform. There was no rest
for her at home. At the full table her
supper, hungry as she was, had been
taken with difficulty. Sam constantly
hovered near her, not visibly, my
young reader; it would have been a
great comfort to her if he had done so;
but still he was there, almost as really, for he was never out of her mind.
She seemed to see him as he stood on
the wharf waving his cap to them.
What was he doing now? Where was
his supper? Was he afraid there all
alone? Would Tom go for him?

These are only a few of the many
questions which she kept constantly
asking herself, or rather which her
conscience asked her. Rachel's con-

science was beginning to be the mayor of her city, and took her to task for everything that disturbed or destroyed its peace. Now it told her that she was the real cause of all Sam's trouble; not that Sam himself had not been to blame, but she should have taken another and a gentler method of reproving him. If she could only persuade Tom to go back for him what would she not do, what would she not give him! Rachel was very much puzzled; she thought over every treasure she possessed in the world. There were her dolls; there was Ella, the darling, with eyes that would open and shut, he should have her; or Sue, made of rubber, able to cry almost like a real child. Yes, she would take them both and give him his choice, if he would only go back and bring Sam home. She ran to her play-room, and had both dolls hidden under her cape, when she remembered hearing Tom laugh at Eddy for playing with Alice's dolls, and call him "girl-boy;" what should he want of them himself? She put them gladly by, for she loved them dearly, and it was very hard to think of parting with them; but conscience told her that, next to being sorry, trying to make amends was the quickest and surest way of repairing broken walls. The reparation, or sacrifice on her part for the sake of making amendment, was giving up her dolls; but if Tom did not want them, and would only laugh at her if she offered them to him, why, then, they were safe, and they might really be hers still.

Books? She had already quite a library, which her parents had given her; but these Tom called "girl's trash." He had said that very day, when she was telling the other children a story she had just read, that he didn't see any fun in such young stuff. When he heard stories he wanted them to be something with a snapper to them; something about shipwrecks, pirates, going to sea, or seeing new countries. He wouldn't give a fig for your home stories about good and bad children; he had quite enough of them every day of his life. All this had made quite an impression upon Rachel as he said it, and now it made the handsome rows of blue, crimson, and gilt books look quite insignificant to her anxious eyes.

While she was in this dilemma her

canaries began to sing. O dear, if
she only could! The thought left
her . eyes full of tears. Could she
give him Nellie? She didn't sing so
much as Dick, and would not be
quite . so sadly missed. But then
there were the cunning eggs, and by
and by, Nancy said, Nell would have
some little tiny birds to take care of.
Dear me! no; Tom would like them.
He came almost every day to see
them, and hear them sing; but she
could not, could not; and Rachel's
tears streamed down so fast that they
quite hid the cage from her view.

"The dearer you love them the
more reparation you will make," said
her conscience.

"Dear! dear! dear!" said Rachel,
wringing her hands, "I can't, I can't,
O dear, I can't!"

"Then you are not truly sorry," said that troublesome conscience again. "If you were, you would be willing to give anything to get Sam safely home."

"I am sorry, I am;" and I am afraid if conscience had been a child standing by Rachel's side, notwithstanding her sorrow, she felt so troubled at the thought of parting with her birds she might have easily repented of the offense of growing angry and striking the child.

"There," said conscience promptly, "don't you see you are only sorry for Sam's suffering and not because you did wrong? You feel as if it was mean in you to be so comfortable here while he is there all alone. You regret this more than you do your sin."

"O I don't, I don't," groaned Ra-

14

chel, soothing herself down; "what shall I do? I can't do right any way, and I can't part with my birds, and I can't have poor Sam there alone all the long, long night. O I am so unhappy!"

"You must give up your birds, then, that will make you happier at once. Try it and see."

"Will it?" and Rachel lifted up her head and looked again toward the cage. Nell was putting her head far out between the wires, chirping in her pretty way, as if she wanted to ask what made her young mistress so sad, and Dick, standing on one foot, was singing his evening song. She remembered how often Nancy had told her this was a way God had given the birds of saying their prayers; and she wished Dick only knew how wrong she had acted, and would ask God to forgive her, and bring Sam home without any more trouble to her, or without making her think she ought to give up her birds. While Rachel was going through all this discipline, which was a part of what God had assigned to her in this trial-world, it was fast growing dark out of doors. Her mamma had friends from Boston staying with her, and she was busy with them in the parlor. On such occasions Rachel had generally gone with Nancy to see the sick person, and Mrs. Tilton, knowing that Nancy was away, and not seeing Rachel, supposed she had gone too, so the child was left to do as she pleased. It was against her mother's express command that she should leave the yard after dark. Never having been near the sea before, Rachel had found it almost impossible to go home and be shut up in the house while it was calling her from the beach within sight of her bedroom window. So when they first came to the island she had left home at a late hour without leave, and after some anxious search she had been found on the shore, sitting to watch the stars come up out of the sea. At that time her mother forbade her going out again after tea unless she was with Nancy.

We must do Rachel the justice to say that in the hurry and trouble of her feelings she forgot this, and it is always so. One sin makes way for so many others. The saying is that "misery loves company," and I think it is so with sins. You give one ad-

mittance and another is sure to follow. This is an important thing,
which I very much wish to make im-
pressive. You may think that this
one little thing which you are about
to do is so very little that it is quite
unimportant. Far from it; this little
thing is hand in hand with another,
perhaps a greater, and you cannot
tell where or how the harm will end.
Rachel saw now that it was fast
growing dark. Whatever she did
must be done quickly. At this moment Zaid came in at the door, and
seeing her began to purr very loudly,
in order to say how glad she was to
see her after her long absence. She
came to her, rubbed her soft white
sides against her, lifted her tail, as if
asking her to use it for a handle and
take her into her arms, and stared up

into her face with her green cat's eyes with as intelligent a look as a kitten can well have.

"O Zaid! Zaid! you will do, I know you will, you darling, precious, precious kit;" and Rachel caught her up, covered her with kisses, and hugged her so close that, in spite of her unwillingness to hurt her little mistress, she had to put out a pretty sharp claw in self-defense ; but Rachel did not feel it. She would not give herself a minute in which to think; Tom should have Zaid all his own, she never would ask him to give it back; he might take it home and keep it forever if he only would go for poor Sam. Going out at the garden gate, she ran off with all speed, carrying Zaid toward the spot where the raft was moored. She had not thought

but that Tom would be waiting for
her; but when she found only the
lonely shore, and the raft dancing up
and down on the water, she felt dis-
appointed. Where was he? how
could she waste the time to hunt him
up? and the light in the western sky
was fading out fast, she saw that
plainly. No child stops to think
long when it has anything to do; certainly Rachel did not now. Zaid
mewed most emphatically several
times to tell her that she was hurting
her; but it did not matter, she hardly heard her; it was only of finding
Tom that she thought. She was going to his house, running very fast,
and out of breath, when he called
her. He had not dared to go home,
for he very well knew if he did that his
mother would send him back at once

for Sam; and though, in truth, he
meant to return, yet he did not wish
to do so until he had given Sam a
good fright, which would make him
more manageable for the future. So
he had staid around in the woods,
where he thought he should not be
very likely to be found. And in
order to make good his words that
the raft should not go back to the
island to-night he intended to take the
boat, which, though old, (his father
had taken the new one,) was sound
and sea-worthy, if well-managed. His
mother never liked to have him use
this; Tom knew it, and as he loved
his mother, he almost always did, in
this respect, as she wished. But Tom
had been hasty, and acted unkindly
to-night, and, as we have already said,
it is the way things always go; after

sin some other wrong act follows.
When he saw Rachel he wondered
where she could be going at such
an unusual hour, and what for, and it
was his curiosity that made him stop
her.

"O Tom," she said, "are you here?
I am so very, very glad. Here is
Zaid, and you may have her for your
own if you will go right over and
bring Sam home."

So great had been Rachel's sacrifice; so fast had her heart beaten, as
she had pressed Kitty against it as
she came; so many tears were waiting
all ready to flow, that she spoke very
indistinctly, and Tom could not tell
what she was saying, until he peeped
into the bundle, which was wrapped
up in the corner of her cape, and saw
the white kitten.

"What are you going to do with that?" he asked.

"Give her to you, if you will only bring Sam home."

What a loud, hearty laugh Tom laughed; it really frightened Rachel, so that, excited as she was, she began to tremble.

"I wouldn't give a copper for all the kittens there are on Nelson's Island," he said bluntly. "Now, if it was a pup you might hire me; but a cat, what on earth do you suppose I could do with a cat? Why, they are for girls; who ever knew a boy care a pin for one?"

Now Rachel did cry, not aloud, boisterously, as Alice did when Tom troubled her, but with great tears rolling one after another down her cheeks as fast as they could. She made no sound, and Tom watched her for a moment in silence.

"What are you crying for?" he said at last; "do you want to get rid of the kitten? I can drown her for you if you do."

Drown Zaid! The very enormity of the proposition seemed to give Rachel courage, and she sobbed out:

"O Tom! Tom! if you would let me keep her I should be so happy."

"Keep her! of course you may; what on earth do you suppose a fellow like me wants to do with a cat?"

Rachel felt as if a great weight had been taken off her, for it must be confessed just now she had forgotten Sam in her grief at parting with Zaid. She made kitty scratch and mew many times before she stopped caressing her, and then she suddenly recollected.

" But will you go for Sam ?"

"Sam! O that is a different thing. He must learn to mind the governor, or, you see, we shall have nothing but law-breaking on the Island, and that wont do. But, say, did you come way over here and bring your cat to give me, all for Sam ?"

" Yes," said Rachel.

" Jolly! you are a girl what is a girl! I like that now. It shows real grit in you."

" What is that ?"

" O, don't you know ? Well, never you mind, you will find out soon enough or I lose my guess ;" and Tom looked admiringly at the child as she stood there in the deepening twilight.

"Come, now, I will tell you what I will do, because it's cute in you, and shows if you have temper you can be sorry for it. Aunt Lee tells us often that it is the noblest thing in the world to say you are sorry if you have injured any one, and I think she is right, because it's the hardest. Now you have been and gone and done it. You haven't said it, but you have acted it, and that is a heap better."

Rachel did not understand all that Tom meant. She only felt that he was good-natured, and that perhaps she might accomplish her object if she would persist.

"You will go for Sam, then," she said hopefully.

"I don't know. Will you go with me?"

"Yes."

"Come on, then."

The two children went together down to a cove at some distance from that in which the raft was moored, and found the old boat partly drawn up on shore. She was half full of water.

"We shall have to bail," said the tired boy, as he looked down into it. For the first time since he had left the island he wished he had brought Sam with them.

"Is that much work?"

"Yes, when a fellow is as tired as a dog, and has only a pint dipper to bail with; but I don't see any help." So Tom picked up a tin dish, which had been previously used for that purpose, and began the task. Rachel watched him a moment in silence, then she said, "There is an old tin pan in the wreck. I will run for it, it will hold more than that."

"That's cute; don't let the grass grow under your feet."

Rachel had no need to be told to be quick in this odd way. She was tired too, but she did not think of it, and it seemed, even to impatient Tom, but a very short time before she came running back with two tin pans in her hand. "That is the kind of girl I like," he said to himself; "she is worth half a dozen like Alice. I declare she is better than Ernest, and I thought he was pretty well up."

Together the boy and girl soon cleared the water from the boat, and though the late summer twilight had entirely gone before they were ready to start, still the stars came out so bright, and the water looked so white and pretty, with its little night-caps of foam, that Rachel felt no fear as she jumped into the boat and Tom pushed off.

She had never before been on the water in the evening, and now, having her heart relieved by the knowledge that Sam would soon be with her, and her conscience by the expiation which she felt she had made in being willing to give away her precious cat, she felt really happy, and quite enjoyed the scene. The low evening song of the mighty ocean might indeed have been pleasant to other and older children. Then there was the clear, starlit sky, the soft rocking motion of the waves, and the freshness, the almost fragrance with which the air was filled. How sweetly the billows came and went, never still, never still. There was something in the ceaseless motion which alone would have been charming to a child.

Tom usually sang as he rowed. He knew several pretty boat songs; but to-night he was silent. In truth, he was too weary to care for anything but accomplishing the object of the trip and then going to bed, so he sat silent.

Zaid went to sleep in Rachel's arms, the best compliment she could pay to the evening's sail.

When they reached the island, Tom called Sam several times in a very loud voice, hoping the child would hear him and would come down and save him the trouble of going on shore; but no Sam answered. Rachel called too. No reply. A little alarmed, Tom left the boat in

Rachel's care and sprang on the wharf. What if something had happened? Tom felt his heart stop beating as he asked himself this question. All at once the fondness which he really felt for his brother rushed over him. He did not think of his faults, of the many times in which he had been annoyed by him. All that he remembered was he heard no answer to his call, and perhaps—but that *perhaps* was too hard to be endured, and Tom thrust it away from him with a great effort. So it will be with you, my readers. If you are ever unkind to your brothers or sisters there will come a time when you will not wish to remember it, but will try to put it away. Tom was a very short time going to the house. Here he thought most probably Sam would take refuge, and here he found him asleep, curled up on the pile of cloths which had served for the partitions, and which he had so mischievously torn down.

At first Tom had a horrible fear that he was dead, he slept so soundly, and gave so little heed to any of his attempts to rouse him. But at last he started with a scream which alarmed Tom almost as much as his silence. It was some time before Tom could waken him to a full sense of where he was, and that he had come to take him home.

Rachel sat in the boat trying to look through the darkness and see if they were not coming. She heard the scream, and seizing the oars, pushed the boat a little way from shore, dropping Zaid on the bottom as she did so; but in a moment she heard Tom's voice.

"Wake up old fellow, can't you? Why you reel about here like a drunken man. There, that is it. Want to take hold of my hand? So you may. Why, you shake as if you were cold. You aint frightened now, with me along, are you? and here is Rachel and her kitten. Come, wake up; we'll have you home in a jiffy, see if we don't."

Tom's voice was very gentle, almost tender. Rachel had never heard it sound so before, and she wondered as she listened.

"Here we are; row up, Rachel; what in nature are you out there for! I say, if that isn't gay, to think Sam and I could step down into the water to you; why it's five miles deep, I dare say."

Rachel brought the boat quickly back, the boys jumped on board, and much more quickly than they came over, for the wind was in their favor, they made their way to Nelson's Island.

Tom told Sam, who had been silent ever since he was wakened, to go directly home, while he went round with Rachel, and without waiting to be spoken to a second time, Sam disappeared. His mother received him as if his coming was a matter of course. He was often out as late with Tom, and always had come back safely, so she never gave herself any trouble about him. She little knew what a tempest of feeling the little fellow had passed through since she saw him last, and it was not until a long time after that he summoned courage to tell any one.

As Rachel came near home she remembered, for the first time, how disobedient she had been. She had been gone from home nearly two hours, but as Nancy had not yet returned, she had not been missed. Mrs. Tilton was, therefore, very much surprised when she opened the door of her room, and coming straight to her said:

"Mamma, I have disobeyed you, and I am very sorry; I forgot all about it, I was so busy thinking of Sam."

"What have you done, my darling?" said her mother, putting her arm affectionately around her.

"I have been with Tom over to the island since dark."

Here followed a long conversation, which, as it would be only a repetition of what we have already said, it is not necessary to detail to the reader. Suffice it to say, Mrs. Tilton felt that she never loved Rachel better than when, after a full confession on her part, she knelt down with her, and begged God to strengthen the walls of her city, and set sharp watchmen around upon it, that none of these harmful, unbidden guests might enter.

CHAPTER X.

CAPTAIN LEE'S RETURN.

THE early summer sun waited a long time the next morning for the "shipwrecked mariners" to make their appearance. The unusual fatigue and excitement of the day before had made them sound and late sleepers, and when, at last, one after the other made their appearance down by the shore, they were tired, sleepy looking children, seeming not to care very much whether the raft left her moorings for all the live-long day.

Tom, too, had lost much of his interest in the new home; it is so true that the spirit of happiness to the young is in doing right. The cloud, not bigger than a man's hand, that can cover their whole heaven, is what may seem at the time the smallest sin. Tom was tired of the authority which brought him so much trouble· and some repentance. He began to think the children too young to play with, and to wish John was back from sea, or that some bigger children would drop down on the island. The consequence was that when the lagging mariners were all ready for embarkation, Rachel with a larger basket than she had brought before, and every one with hands full of articles which were to supply some discovered necessity, Tom told them he had changed his mind, and instead of going to the island he was going down to the cove to fish.

There was no denying his right to do as he pleased; so, after some consultation among themselves, they determined to spend the day upon the wreck, picnicing there, instead of doing so at their new home.

The day was not more than half through, a very quiet, happy day it was, in which they all agreed, told stories, played at housekeeping, and each one took pains to be obliging and kind to the others, when the shell sounded from Mrs. Lee's house, and Ernest ran to see what their mother wanted.

A letter had just been brought from their father, in which he wrote, that having determined not to go to the port which made the extreme length of his journey, he had already set sail for home, and might be expected in a very few days after the arrival of the steamer which would bring this letter. What a time of rejoicing it was, how quickly the children flew from one house to another, telling the good news, and how little else was talked of or thought of that day, those of my readers who have learned to love Captain Lee may imagine.

In their delight they even forgot the party which they had intended to get up on the little island for his reception, and it was not until gravely reminded of it by Tom after his return at night from his fishing excursion, that they began to feel how much remained to be done. For several successive days they went regularly to the island, worked with much concord and earnestness, and when at last the white sails of the ship rose above that distant horizon beneath which they last disappeared, every-thing was in readiness.

Tom's raft had been lying at the island, on the side toward the harbor, waiting for this signal, and now, amid a universal rejoicing which made it rather unsafe for such young voyagers, it was crowded with the children and headed toward the ship. It had not gone far when they saw the ship drop anchor, a boat lowered, and two persons run down the side.

"There's father! there's uncle! there's John! Hurrah! Now for it, three times three cheers;" and the raft tipped quite into the water as the boys stamped and clapped and cheered at the same time. Back from the boat came an answering call, and very soon the two crafts were along-

side, and Alice, without much regard
to the deep water which rolled between them, sprang into her father's
arms.

The children must all come on
board the boat; the practiced eye of
the sea-captain saw at once that joy
and rafts were not very safe compan-
ions under children's guidance; so
Tom and John were left to row the
raft in, while the homeward bound
boat, under the long, steady pulls of
the captain, soon outstripped it, and
came into port.

Our readers must imagine all the
details of the return, how happy
Mrs. Lee's home was that night, and
how much pleasure it gave their father to see the growth and improve-
ment of Ernest and Alice during his
absence. Nor can we find room in

this volume, which is already too long, to relate the particulars of the party which took place in due time upon the little island: we will only say everything passed off to the delight of all concerned.

The great secret of the children was revealed to those at home, from whom it had been faithfully and carefully kept, and Nancy won from Tom the praise of being able to keep a secret right smart if she was a woman.

Mrs. Tilton and Captain Lee were old friends, and the addition of the little. orphan Rachel to her family met with his warmest approbation and praise.

"To think of it," said the good captain, with tears dimming his kind blue eyes, "that God should have sent us both to the same place, and we should have taken these dear children to bring them up as it were together on this island;" and then, as he ran his eye over the group of children, a sudden thought seemed to strike him.

"I'll tell you what it is," he said, "this shall be a kind of branch Orphan Asylum. That nice Scotch boy, what do you call him, Rachel? the light-haired, blue-eyed fellow, with a whole summer of sunshine hidden away somewhere within his laughing face; the one that put on my hat, you know?"

"Christie," said both Rachel and Ernest together.

"Yes, that's the one; well now, children, I guess we must manage some way to get him down here too;

pretty nice that would be, wouldn't
it ?"

"Yes, sir," said both children eagerly.

"·So it would; we will think it over
and let you know when we decide,"
and the captain's face had at once the
look which it always wore when he
was thinking it over.

He held a long consultation that
night with his wife and Mrs. Tilton,
the result of which we shall make
known in our next volume, called
" Christie ; or, Where the Tree Fell."
We must now leave our party of
children.

Tom was very much pleased to
have done with the little folks, and
to be able to join in the more manly
sports of his elder brother John.

Sam was still plotting, and still not

to be trusted, getting himself and other people into trouble, and never learning the great life-lesson that honesty, even in trifles, is by far the best policy, to say nothing of its being the only life pleasing to a spirit-searching God.

Ernest, with no marked faults, and a strong desire to do right, was quick-tempered and impulsive, and still went wrong sometimes because he would not stop to think.

Alice, selfish and sullen by fits, succeeded at last in remembering the prayer that she might be generous, loving, and loved.

Little Eddy took the coloring of whatever atmosphere he was in, happy when the others were happy, sorry when they were sorry, good when they were good, and naughty when

16

they were naughty; but we must not forget that Eddy was only a very little boy, and he would have more character as he grew older.

As for Rachel, what shall we say of the walls of her city? Certainly, they were not yet safe from all assaults of the enemy. Almost every day of her life there were times when they shook to their foundations, times when she forgot to shut her gates, times when the good mayor within warned and invited and plead with her to do so; but she turned a deaf ear to all that was said. The most difficult enemy still to deal with was the violent temper; but Rachel was learning the value of prayer, was learning that the only way to show her earnestness in what she asked was to live up to the light that she had. Poor little Rachel!

there is a lesson in her life for each one of you, my young readers. Have you not discovered it? Are there none of you that will be more watchful to rule over your own spirit, so that your city may not be broken down and without walls?

THE END.